D1806334

Appointment in
# Puerto Banus
Marbella
"Double Abduction"

The story in this book is the result of the author's
imagination

Printed and bound by blurb.com
PO Box 728, San Francisco CA 94104-0728
First published in paperback in 2012

# ____Dedication____

The disgusting and dark world of sex trafficking is big business with many authorities trying to stop it, but without much success, it would appear.

I have  dedicated this book to all those poor unfortunate youngsters who have been trafficked throughout the world. The world must never forget their pleight.
May their God be with them.

Jon Grainge

# "An Appointment"
Series of paperback books
Also available as an E-BOOK with Blurb.com

# Appointment in **Puerto Banus**    *"Double Abduction"*

**Map of Marbella and Puerto Banus**

# Appointment in **Puerto Banus**     "Double Abduction"

# Appointment in

# Puerto Banus

## Marbella

## " Double Abduction"

another action-Adventure novel by

# Jon Grainge

# _____Preface_____

Melika and Leyla Demir, two of the most beautiful Anglo-Indian sisters you can imagine, go on a holiday to the glamorous resort of **Marbella** in Southern Spain and find themselves as guests of the owner of a super yacht, the *"Ria Jocoba"*. Whilst on a short trip aboard the boat, the situation changes and they end up in Casablanca, Morocco where their lives become a commodity for sale to the highest bidder from the Algerian MAFIA ..

Can they escape or do they have to settle for a life of sex slavery?

Does this trade exist today? To my greatest regret and shame I would suggest it does!

# Appointment in **Puerto Banus**          "Double Abduction"

Chapter 1.
_____**All excited.**

Chapter 2.
_____**"Banus control Ria Jocoba here"**

Chapter 3
_____**In Spain we are!**

Chapter 4
_____**Hola Espana**

Chapter 5
_____ **Nikki Beach**

Chapter 6
_____**Appointment in Banus**

Chapter 7
_____**Partytime**

Chapter 8
_____**Entry into Casablanca**

Chapter 9
_____**Hell in Casablanca**

Chapter 10
_____**The Auction Approaches**

Chapter 11
_____**Let the Selling Begin**

Appointment in
# Puerto Banus
## Marbella

"Double Abduction"

# The tip of Southern Spain and Morocco

**Chapter 1**
_____ **All Excited**

The scene in the sitting room of 33b Phaeton St, London was one of pandemonium with the two sisters, Melika and Leyla Demir, hurriedly doing last minute packing for their trip to Marbella in the morning. Being the first time they have been away abroad together without their parents, the two stunningly beautiful twins of eighteen years old were really excited and looking forward to their first adventure together in the sun.

*"Should I take this blue bikini Leyla or wait till will get there and buy one in the market?"* Melika asked.

*"Take the blue one just in case you cannot find a better one there"* was Leyla's reply.

*"Just remind me dear sister what's the name of our hotel?"* Leyla asked.

*" Let me see. Ah here we are , it's the Fuerte "* Melika replied as she pulled the wallet containing  train tickets and hotel reservation from her wheelie case.

*"Let's hope they have a good bar so we can meet some good looking dudes to have some fun with"* she continued.

By this time the room in the rather tatty two bedroomed apartment, in the not too salubrious area of Hackney, was in total disarray with clothes adorning every piece of furniture with shoes and cosmetics strewn over the floor.

Both girls, having been brought up in outer suburbs of Leicester, were of Indian origin but had spent the majority of their lives in Leicestershire where they manifested the want to both become fashion models. Having left school they contacted Beauty Shooters model agency in the West-End of London and following an initial visit/casting to the agency office were immediately signed up by the boss, Jonny Grainge. Obviously living up north and working down south would prove to be unpractical, hence with a little financial help from Mum and Dad, the two beauties rented the second floor apartment in Phaeton St. It was a small terraced, furnished dwelling of a standard that was somewhat less than they had been used too up north, but it was comfortable and affordable. They were happy with it.

It had been roughly six months since they had moved in and had worked on several successful shows and photo-shoots in the London area, during that summer. Now, being September, they jointly felt like a break in the sun to build up a natural winter tan for upcoming winter assignments they had been retained for through the agency.

Jonny , the agency boss who had spent much of his life in southern Spain in his illustrious career, had recommended Marbella as it was one of the few places in Europe that had guaranteed sun at that time of the year.

*"What time do you think we should leave for St Pancras in the morning?"* Leyla further asked.

*"Well , the train departs at 0730am so allowing for the taxi I would suggest 0600am. How does that sound?"*

*"Ok so we had better book a taxi now ."* Leyla suggested.

Some two hours then passed before the bulging cases were finally packed and their padlocks clipped shut. When young ladies travel it is usual for them not to travel light, Melika and Leyla were no exception but as they were to be travelling on the high-speed  Eurostar, TGV and AVE trains which carry no weight restriction, this was to be to their advantage.

*"Let's have a drink before turning in"* Leyla suggested as she walked across the room to the kitchen where the vodka was stored in the carousel.

Once she had located a couple of highball glasses from the cupboard and quarter filled them with the Smirnoff Red vodka plus a couple of cubes of ice from the fridge freezer, she strolled over to Melika,

*"Cheers sis. Here's to a successful holiday and hope we get laid at least once."*
*"Cheers."*
Melika having a liking to alcohol, especially Vodka, downed it in one!
With both glasses now empty it was agreed that they would go to their beds.
Leyla was the first to hear the bedside alarm, which read 0515am when she depressed the cancel button,
*"Wakey, wakey Melika time to get up"* shouted Leyla as she knocked on her bedroom door. No reply.
*"Melika are you awake!"* Leyla voiced as she opened the door only to find her twin sister snoring away. The Vodka had taken it's effect. Dragging the sheet off the bed, exposing the naked Melika curled up in a foetal position with her left hand snugly embedded between her upper thighs, Leyla shook her sister's shoulders,
*"Come on wake up sis time to get ready."*
Slowly, very slowly, the static body came to life.
*"Is it time to rise already? I was having such a wonderful dream about someone I met in Marbella Ley."*
*"I can see that! Now come on and get dressed the taxi will be here in forty minutes"* and off she went to have a quick wash and apply some basic make-up.
Standing in front of the large mirror hanging above the basin , Leyla caught glimpse of the

reflection of her beautifully formed 34b-24-35 naked body adorned by her wonderfully conditioned auburn hair resting on her shoulders, then using her  piercing green  eyes to further wander over her breasts and appreciate the pert erect nipples that the cold water had just made contact with,

*"Pretty damn good. That must be of interest to someone on the holiday"* she quietly thought to herself. Just at that point of self adoration in walked the still naked Melika. Looking in the mirror, excepting for the small mole sited a few inches above Melika's right breast , one would be pushed to tell who was who as their similarity was uncanny.

Despite them being indistinguishable from each other in looks, their taste in clothes could not be further diverse as a few minutes later there stood Melika in her smart open white, see-thru blouse and green micro mini skirt, proudly portraying her great pair of legs to the world, with a pair of recently purchased green stilettos , whilst Leyla preferred to travel in her yellow tank top , black leggings and black stilettos.

*"Are you going to wear a coat Mel?"*

*"Well I suppose we ought to take something. What about taking our shawls?"*

*"Sounds sensible."*

Suddenly the intercom buzzer emitted its loud shrill.

*"Must be the taxi"* Leyla shouted with excitement as she ran to lift the receiver,

*"Hello."*
*"Taxi for a Miss Demir."*
*"Thankyou we will be right down."*
Now the girls had a last minute rush around
*"Passports, tickets, money, hotel reservation, blackberry. They're all here"*
Melika remarked as she placed them into the front pocket of her wheelie bag.
*"Come on . Let's go."*
The driver was patiently seated in the black cab when they stepped on to the pavement before manoeuvring themselves into the rear of the car. Melika leant forward,
*"St Pancras station please."*
Neither of the girls had been to St Pancras since it's recent sympathetic renovation, incorporating twenty first century designs and materials within the original Victorian architecture, to become the UK hub for Eurostar's high-speed trains to the continent, it has become the most sofisticated and modern terminus in Britain, complete with it's many classy shops, cafes and the longest champagne bar in Europe.
As they walked through the imposing Victorian entrance into the buzzing throng within, Melika stood back in awe at the presentation,
*"How could this be a railway station?"* she remarked to her sister *"It's fantastic! Makes Leicester's interior look like its from the third world."*
Taking note of the information displayed on the

electronic departure board it did not take long for them to escort their matching Revelation wheelie bags to the Eurostar check-in desk where a smartly dressed young man requested sight of their tickets and passports.

*"You are on the 0727 to Paris, seats 2b and 2c in carriage 17. Please pass through to security and have a good journey."*

Despite the queue the Demir sisters had a smooth and swift passage through the x-ray gate and baggage inspection machine  into the pillared waiting area with it's beautifully polished walnut floor and white steel columns.

Whilst quietly seated awaiting the platform door to open Leyla could not help to state the obvious,

*"Why the hell can't airports be as quick and easy as this Mel?"*

*"Beats me sis. I agree this is fantastic. So far your favourite photographer's suggestion to go by train instead of flying is well founded."*

Soon the vast waiting room became full to capacity with passengers patiently awaiting to board the 0727. Most were either smart gentlemen in suits with their computer cases slung over their shoulders off to Paris for a day's business or well groomed ladies complete with their empty shoulder or wheelie bags in anticipation of a good day's shopping in the Champs Elysee before catching one of the evening services back to London. It was noticeable that Leyla felt a little out of place in her leggings.

*"Ladies and gentlemen. The 0727 to Paris is about to depart so please make your way to platform 2"* came across the tannoy at which point the automatic doors at the far ends of the room opened allowing access to the platform above via several ascending escalators.

Alighting from the top of the steel stairs and coming face to face with the yellow and grey monster of a machine that was to carry them to Paris was the point when the full excitement of the journey to Spain sank in resulting in Melika jumping up and down in excitement, much to the amusement of fellow passengers, who through their own regular use of Eurostar just saw this as a normal train journey.

No sooner had they stowed the cases and sat down in the brown striped seats the train, dead on time, gently eased it's way forward from under the glass and steel roof, into the dim morning sunlight of north London. This view was soon to change as disappointingly the train entered a tunnel which would not reveal daylight until the Eurostar was leaving the suburbs of south London when it would pick up speed as it engaged the true HS1 track. Once through Ebbsfleet the speed rapidly built up to Eurostar's full one hundred and eighty five miles per hour. Both the girls were so impressed with the trains smooth and quiet passage through, the now sunny, Kent countryside until they could feel the deceleration as Eurostar approached the Channel

Tunnel where it's speed has to be reduced to one hundred miles per hour for it's underwater transition.

In no time at all the French daylight came streaming through the windows when once again full speed was attained and  held for the full distance to the outskirts of Paris, some one hour later.

The terminus for Eurostar in Paris is the Gare du Nord, which unlike the glitz and glamour of St Pancras, retains the old style parisien ambience about it.

Gradually Eurostar came to a halt at one of the central platforms whereupon all the passengers wrestled to the doors. Melika and Leyla, knowing they had an hour or so to get to the Gare de Lyon to catch the French TGV to Madrid, sat and waited for the carriage to empty before locating their bags and disembarking with ease.

*"Yippee we are in Paris!"* Melika yelled. Never having been there before she now felt truly abroad.

Feeling buzzy and confident they made their way to the metro where the booking agent in London advised them to go, find platform 4 for Port d'Orleans and change at Chaterlet onto line 14. The first stop would be Gare de Lyon. What seemed just like a few minutes they were both alighting into the huge open space of the station where they were surprised at just how many high speed TGV trains were awaiting their passengers.. On leaving London Leyla had only seen one other train unit  but here in Paris there had to be twenty.

*"Have you the ticket voucher sis?"* Leyla asked *"Remember we have to get the full ticket from the office over there."*

Fumbling in her wheelie Melika produced the documents and over to the small sales queue they both wandered.

*"Your train leaves platform 3 at 1410 hrs"* the ticket salesgirl said in broken English, as she handed Leyla the tickets.

With a several minutes to spare they took the opportunity to view the station and admire the advanced look of the trains over what they knew in UK before making tracks to gate 3 where the LED board indicated that their train was now boarding.

As the girls ambled through the platform gate they heard,

*"Mademoiselle, ici"* as the inspector pointed at the yellow ticket stamping machine. Both had forgotten to have the tickets stamped as instructed by the London agent.

The huge, gleaming bullet shaped, SNCF TGV (Tren a Grande Vitesse) in blue and silver livery with 703 painted on it's nose was  stood there poised ready to accept it's passengers bound for Lyon, Montpellier, Perpignan, Barcelona and Madrid in Spain. It had only been weeks since the link up between the French and Spanish networks was completed making the twins amongst the first passengers on this new and historical high speed cross border route..

For the second time that day the girls took their seats only for this time on a much longer journey, around six hours in fact.  No sooner had they sat down on the plush grey seats when Leyla noticed the platform gently slipping by. The train was so smooth that it's motion could not be detected from onboard . The acceleration was impressive and before long the TGV was speeding through the Parisien outskirts and out into the french countryside at two hundred and twenty miles per hour.

Both  girls agreed that Eurostar was smooth, but then this TGV was something else. To pass the time they even manged to balance an upright ten pence coin on the table without it falling over! Some engineering. The neat and tidy fields of the bountiful farms sped  on and on mesmorising Leyla as she continually gazed out of the window. It was difficult to appreciate the distance the TGV was covering, In what seemed like a few minutes to the entranced Leyla (but in actual fact it was nearer one and a half hours) the train began to decelerate as it approached France's second city - Lyon. The stop at Lyon was brief , as dictated by the philosophy of high-speed travel, and with an assortment of some additional passengers the TGV once again drew speed as it absorbed electrical feed from the overhead cantilevers through it's pantographs.

All the way from Paris the seats opposite the girls had been unoccupied but now, following the pick-up's in Lyon the window seat was now taken up by a smart young Frenchman, in his late forties, attired in a light grey suit and would appear to be on a business trip as he had stowed his Louis Vuitton, designer leather briefcase in the overhead shelf. Leyla, having a soft spot for older men especially if they emitted the appearance of wealth and compounded with the onsetting boredom of the journey, began to plot a bit of fun! Turning to Melika, who by now was beginning the onset of forty winks,

*"Mel, wake up Mel"* Leyla whispered into her ear.

*"What is it?"*

*"What do you think of this guy opposite?"* Leyla asked.

Not wishing to be disturbed from her ensuing slumber Melika replied,

*"Yes he's ok"* and fell back asleep.

Leyla calculated that the time to Montpellier was around thirty minutes and Perpignan an hour, just time for a bit of flirting, but first she should ascertain where he was going to be a game for a laugh, so leaning across the table she spoke,

*"Excuse me, have you the time?"*

*"Oui. It's 4.10pm"* he replied.

*"So you speak English then?"* she then said.

*"Of course."*

*"Where are you going?"* Leyla then asked.

*"Barcelona and you?"* he responded. More than enough time she thought to herself!

*"Madrid and then onto Marbella."*

*"Holiday I guess then?"* he asked.

*"Yes. This is my twin sister and we are fashion models in London."*

*"I see. You are both very beautiful girls"* he replied in a typical french tone.

*"My name is Leyla. What is yours?"* she asked.

*"Francois."*

It was becoming obvious to the intelligent and married frenchman that Leyla was 'playing'. Why else would such a pretty young girl be asking these questions of a complete stranger. He did not object, although as a happily married man, - he should. The temperature was mounting so Francois took off his jacket  carefully laying it on the seat next to him. It was then, as his unjacketed body disturbed the air, that Leyla got a whiff of his perfume .. she loved a good man's fragrance .. that was it. Her mind was made up and was now determined to weald the power she knew she held over men.

*"Fancy buying me a drink in the bar, Francois?"* she asked leaning on the table with her elbows whilst gently blinking her eyebrows at him.

*"Ok"* and off they went leaving Melika to her dreaming blissfully unaware of their absence.

*"Apres-vous, sorry after you"* he directed as the inter-connecting carriage door automatically opened. What a gentleman she thought. Now she was really turned on! so much so that as they passed the toilet, displaying

'vacant', Leyla opened the door, walked inside and turned to Francois,

*" Coming in then?"*

Standing back in amazement whilst supporting a look of total lustful surprise Francois could not believe his luck, however, he resisted,

*"No, sorry. A drink and a chat is fine to pass the time, but no more"* he stated and continued on towards the bar. Not used to having her advances thwarted Leyla followed him to the bar with her tail between her legs. The hour they spent together passed with pleasant conversation.

The journey continued as the TGV briefly stopped at the port town of Montpellier in Provence and Perpignan. Soon they were across the Spanish border and plundering towards Barcelona at the full two hundred and twenty miles per hour again. All the way from Montpellier only small talk prevailed between the girls, however, Leyla had surrepticiously been planning a little idea in her mind for a little more fun when they got to Marbella.

Chapter 2
_____"**Banus control Ria Jacoba here**"


*"Banus control. This is M.V. Ria Jocoba requesting a visitors berth for three days. Over."*

*" Ria Jocoba, welcome back. What is your size and type, over"* was the reply from the duty officer in the Capitania of the prestigious Puerto Banus marina located just west of Marbella.

*"Banus control. We are twin screw motor cruiser of thirty five metres, over"* responded Captain Fallah.

*"Ria Jocoba. Permission granted. Will you moor on row 1 , no. 106 please, over."*

*"Banus control will do, out."*

The experienced suntanned, Moroccan in his early forties then picked up the internal telephone and pressed the button marked 'owners cabin' and awaited the responce.

*"Jamouri."*

*"Sir, we have permission to enter"* Fallah informed his boss in a positive but nervous pitch.

*"Good. Inform me when we are docked, captain."*

Youssef Jamouri, an overweight Moroccan was a bad man, well known within the precinct of his Algerian Mafia friends as " The Hood." An affluent member of the Casablancan society whose true profession was unknown except  to those important few who had been enlisted on his payroll. The  violent and ruthless reputation of " The Hood" had been earned over the years and never had the police ever come close to arresting him as any evidence applicable to his cases always seen to vanish at the last minute.

Captain Fallah brought the Anaconda 35 gracefully through the marina entrance, past the fuel pier and turned port before stern manoeurving the craft into  mooring 106. Once within a couple of feet of the concrete mooring the other two crew members, Bassir and Lyam jumped ashore to attach the stern ropes to the bollards before picking up the bow leader and trailing it forwards to attach to the boat's forward bollard.

 With "Ria Jocoba" safely moored Captain Fallah closed the throttles before cutting the two M.A.N. turbocharged diesels and then again picked up the telephone,

*"Sir we are safely moored and I am off to check- in at the Capitania."*

*"Excellent. Ask Mohammed to join me"* Jamouri commanded.

*"Very well sir."*

Shortly afterwards there was a distinct but forceful knock on the cabin door,

*"Come in Mohammed"* beckoned Jamouri . The door opened and in walked Jamouri's right hand sidekick, Mohammed Karim. A brute of a

man, Algerian by birth, standing two metres tall, broad in the shoulders and carrying no remorse for the physical damage he had inflicted upon other men and the ocassional woman. The tattoo of a coiled serpent, starting just above the left ear and ending in the middle of his hairy chest, had been long set and was clearly visible under his unbuttoned shirt. Not a man to meddle with unless your back is against the wall.

*"Ah Mohammed come sit down. We need to develop a plan for the next couple of days."*

Chapter 3

## _____In Spain we are

As the TGV came to it's usual undetectable halt in Barcelona's 'Estacio de Sants', Francois retrieved his briefcase from the overhead luggage rack, bid his farewell and thanks to the twins before rapidly disappearing down the carriage to disembark. As he passed the train window      en-route for the station exit Leyla blew him a kiss which he promtly ignorned for fear that the colleague meeting him, might see and report back to his wife.

*"Ah well, only a couple of hours to Madrid so I suppose we will have to settle back and enjoy the passing view"* Leyla commented.

*"Did you enjoy your first french encounter then Mel ?"*

*"Yes not bad. A bit risky though.*

Once leaving the stunning landscape of Barcelona behind the next couple of hours passed quickly and without incident as both girls slept most of the time only to be later awakened by the train's tannoy,

*"Madames et Monsieurs ........ we are approaching Madrid Atocha where this train*

*terminates. Would all passengers prepare to disembark.... merci."*

Madrid is a very large city with a long run in for the train. Nothing much, but houses, to look at. With the train now at rest the girls gathered up their wheelies and disembarked into the vast and extremely busy Atocha Station. The large clock, standing atop it's large brick pillar in the centre of the station, read 8.20pm and outside it was dark although one could not tell that from inside the well lit station.

*"What's the destination of the next train we have to catch Mel?* Leyla asked.

*"Malaga which should be leaving at 9pm."*

*"Good lord look at that Mel!"* Leyla suddenly exclaimed looking to her left.

*"Bloody  hell. Come on let's have a quick look."*

Walking though the central archway they were faced with a "rain forest"! and on further entry into the vast hallway the humidity and temperature rose rapidly to the point that both girls began to sweat heavily. They found themselves amidst a forest of palm and other tropical trees surrouding a central pool full of lily's and tortoise. It was the world famous Puerta de Atocha.

*"What a fantastic display sis. Why can't more stations do things like this?"*

*"C'mon Leyla we cannot waste time looking at trees we must find the platform for our train"* and grabbed her sister's arm pulling

her in the direction of the departure information board.

The 2100hrs (9pm) service AVE (Alta Velocidad Espanola) 3452 from Madrid to Malaga was showing leaving platform 6a and was displaying 'ontime'. Once they had observed the platform, with the beautiful sleek white/mauve train waiting to accept it's payload, Leyla turned to Melika and suggested they find a sandwich or baguette to eat before boarding as she was feeling hungry and was not sure what eating facilities might be onboard.

*"Great idea Leyla. Look over there that look 's like some snacks"* and over they went to the delightful stall offering tapas and pastries.

*"Hola chica's. Tu mucho humbre?"* spoke the young Spaniard.

*"Sorry we are English!"* replied Leyla.

*"Inglis. Oh ok. You hungry?"* he then repeated in his polite attempt at broken English.

*"Yes ."*

*"Try some  this. Is very good"* handing Leyla a couple of gigantic curry pasties .

*"Ok we will have those, thankyou"* Leyla said.

*"Ten euros chica."* He had seen them coming! Melika fumbled in her bag for some of the  euros she had purchased from the local post office in Hackney earlier that week.

*"Muchas Gracias. Hasta Luego"* he bidded them and off the girls ran towards platform 6a. Strolling up the platform alongside the bullet

shaped train seeking out the  most forward access door neither of the sisters could believe the modernity of the design of this spanish beast. It was then that Leyla looked down at the bogie to see a name plate riveted to the lower carriage apron,  ' Built in Germany by Siemens'.

*"Bloody hell. What with the last train built in France and this German built train operating in Spain, how ever far behind has England dropped behind Europe?"* Leyla remarked. *" No wonder Jon recommended we go by train to Marbella."*

Having been lucky enough to have been allocated the second row in the leading carriage which, on the ICE3 design of train, incorporated the drivers cab allowing the passengers a forward view through the glass partition. Once settled in the dark blue leather seats neither of the girls could believe that Spain had such advanced trains. It felt more akin to being in a plane rather than a train!

At exactly 9pm the pneumatic doors closed and AVE 3452 began it's forward motion. Slowly at first until the final carriage had reached the end of the platform before the driver opened the throttle lever when the train lept forward in a surge of electrical acceleration that took the girl's breath away. The outskirts of Madrid simply passed in a blur and with the view of the oncoming track through the partition looking like a speedied up movie. Leyla and Melika sat back to enjoy the experience.

*"Senors y Senoritas. Bienvinedo ... our first stop will be Cordoba and then Malaga. Time to Cordoba is one hour and Malaga is one and a half hours. Enjoy your journey."*

Once the train was clear of Madrid there was nothing for the girls to see through the window into the pitch darkness outside. Even their forward motion at two hundred and forty five miles per hour was undetectable so they embarked on devouring their curry pasties.

*"Wow! That is good. So spicy and tasty"* Leyla commented as she tried to swallow the first bite and talk at the same time

*"Huuum Agreed."*

Once the pasties had been fully consumed the girls decided on forty winks so decided to cuddle together for extra comfort. Their sleep proved to be deep as the stop at Cordoba came and went without them noticing. On entry into the suburbs of Malaga the silence was again  disturbed by the announcement from the tannoy,

*"Senors y Senoritas..... we are approaching Malaga 'Maria Zambrano' station. Would everyone prepare to disembark. .... gracias."*This awoke the slumbering twins who immediately retrieved their wheelie bags from the luggage section of the coach. It was Melika who first spoke,

*"God that was quick. What time is it sis?*
*"10.28pm, Mel."*
*"So at the end of the day not much slower*

*than flying. Jonny was right again"* Melika commented

*"Do you think the taxis will be just outside the station entrance?"* Leyla then asked.

*" I would have thought so. We will soon find out"* Mel replied.

It was not possible to determine the exact point when the train came to it's smooth halt as the passengers lined up by the exit doors awaiting for them to open automatically. Alighting from the train and progressing through the ticket barriers the girls found themselves in the centre of a fantastic shopping centre and despite the late hour all the shops were still open.

*"This is unbelievable sis. There is no station just a shopping centre, but it's so big and the clothes ..it's a dream"* Leyla commented with a modicome of delight and excitement in her delivery.

*"Come on Leyla, stop dreaming we must find the taxi rank and get to the hotel"* and away they went to find the shopping centre entrance. Once outside in the warm evening air the rank of waiting taxis was clearly evident.

*"Go on you ask him Mel"* suggested Leyla as they approached the front Seat Cordoba.

*"Excuse me. Can you take us to the Hotel Fuerte in Marbella please.*

*"Si, no problema chica."*

The fifty mile journey along the coastal N340 and Autovia (motorway),  passing through Fuengirola and Calahonda, took a good hour giving the girls a great chance to see the Costa del Sol at night. From the highest point on the Autovia, above the sprawling town of Arroyo de la Miel, the extensive view of the coast was captivating. Nothing but lights and more lights highlighting the extent of construction and habitation all the way along the Mediterranean coastline. Leyla even spotted the lights of an ocean liner cruising far out to sea on the horizon.

*"Chicas, Hotel Fuerte aqui"* the driver announced as he pulled up outside a rather good looking hotel whose entrance was on the Av. de Ramon y Cajal in central Marbella.

*"How much do we owe you?"* Leyla asked. Assuming his passengers were requesting the price the driver answered,

*"Cien euros par favour.... One hundred."*

*"One hundred euros!!! Shit that's one hundred pounds"* Leyla shouted in disbelief.

*"That's the same as the train fare from Paris to here."*

*"Just pay him sis and let's go and check in. I'm too tired to argue."*

Chapter 4

_____**Hola Espana**

Dawn broke throwing rays of bright Spanish sunlight into the south facing room 310 on the third floor of the Fuerte Hotel.

*"Wakey Mel. Time to get up and see what beautiful Marbella has to offer before we go down to the beach."*

Within an hour both girls had washed, applied make-up and had got dressed, which was quite quick for them.

*"What about breakfast then?"* Melika asked.

*"Let's just go and have a coffee on the seafront in the sun"* Leyla suggested as she was keen to get started on her tan as soon as possible so off they went with Melika having the bag containing the towels and creams slung over her shoulder.

The walk along Av. del Duque de Ahumada, with a cloudless sky, was a pleasant introduction to the delights of Marbella. Both girls in their mini skirts with their bikini's on underneath strolled arm in arm down the clean and presentable street, admiring the view of the beach side shops, the never-ending promenade and the flash sea-view apartments, whilst looking out for a cafe.

*"That look's nice sis. Shall we sit there in the sun?"* Melika suggested. This they did and ordered two coffee's with milk and two pan au chocolat. Whilst enjoying her first taste of Spanish coffee in a glass, which is the traditional way in Spain, Melika cast her eyes towards the billboard mounted on the wall of the shop on the other side of the street,

*"Look Leyla. What about going there?"* she said as she began to read out aloud the gist of the poster, **'Nikki Beach. Party night tonight'** from 9pm , girls free entry.

Immediately Leyla got excited and the more she read the more excited she became,

*"Just what the doctor ordered. We definately must go to that tonight sis. Don't you agree?"*

*"Definately. We will arrange a taxi from the hotel when we get back."*

The coffee and pan au chocolat went down very well afterwhich they made their way further down the attractive avenue to the steps leading down to the crowded horse-shoe shaped beach.The sun was now really begining to promote it's power raising the September air temperature to a very acceptable eighty five or so degrees. Once they had laid out the towels in the chosen spot, off came the dresses and on went the factor

twenty before taking up a lying down position in order to capture as many rays as they could. It did not take long before the bikini top's were removed, after all it would not be good on photos to have white boobs and a tanned chest!
off came the dresses and on went the factor
Naturally every single male that passed them by either gave a 'good' look or a whitty quip in Spanish in the hope of! At this stage the girls were having none of it, they just wanted an all over tan as quickly as possible and nothing was going to get in their way. Even a snack for lunch was forbad as this would interrupt several minutes of tanning! It was not until the sun was drifting toward the evening horizon that the two burnt girls decided that it was time to return to the hotel for a shower and get dressed up for dinner and drinks  at the party at Nikki Beach.

Chapter 5

# _____Nikki Beach

*"Some more champagne sir to wash down the olives and dates?"* asked the steward leaning over Jamouri's shoulder whilst refilling his glass with some more Bollinger '97.

*"Of course. By the way tell chef that the salmon was poached to perfection but the quails eggs were runny and if they are like that again he (the chef) will be poached next time!"* Jamouri threatened.

Suddenly Mohammed stood up, walked across the specially imported carpet, to the aft salon door of the glorious Anaconda 35 metre motor yacht, slid it open and turned back towards to his so called business partner, Jamouri,

*"The car has just pulled on the mooring Youssef."*

*"Ok tell the driver that we will be ten or so minutes."*

Jamouri then stood up and proceeded down the carriageway and main staircase to his master cabin where he unlocked the wall safe and removed five thousand euros in fresh two hundred euro notes which he stuffed into the inside pocket of his cream and beautifully pressed YSL (Yves Saint Laurent) suit. The German made pistol was then slid into the back of the trousers - just in case!

*"Tell Capt Fallah to expect us back around 3-4 am"* he advised the steward brushing past on his way to the aft salon doors and gangplank leading down to the waiting car. The gleaming white Maserati Grand Tourismo four door car, which Jamouri usually hired with a driver from Salamanca Cars of San Pedro, was immaculately turned out, as was the suited driver,

*"Good evening Mr Jamouri. Nice to see you again"* remarked the driver Jose.

*"You too Jose"* as he slipped a two hundred note into his greasy palm. *"You know the drill, same as before, right?"*

*"Yes of course sir."*

Gently the 'Mazzey' approached the entrance barrier of Puerto Banus as it raised allowing access to the N-340 where Jose turned right and depressed the throttle until the needle indicated one hundred and twenty kilometres per hour. It did not take long for the Maserati to cover the eight miles to the Elviria exit at which point Jose pulled off the N340 to pass by the Don Carlos Hotel and down the the beach front where the entrance to Nicci Beach Club was sited.

Having parked at the club's front, the duty staff immediately recognised the Grand Tourismo and it's occupants resulting in the manager being informed, who promtly ran to greet his most generous guest, never realising he was the infamous 'Hood' from the Casablancan Mafia.

*"Good evening sir and once again may I welcome you to Nikki Beach. Would you like your usual table?"* asked Senor Seville.

*"Yes"* was the stern reply. Jamouri was not the most polite or eloquent of men!

The party was in full swing with it's usual international affluent party crowd as Jamouri and Mohammed walked through the 'playing' throng to the white table strategically placed at the bottom of the steps on the edge of the soft brown beach.

*"Drinks? What would you like to drink Sir?"* asked Seville.

*"Champagne, Bollinger. Better make it a magnum with four glasses"* responded Jamouri.

*"Of course sir"* and off went Senor Seville, shortly to return with a steward carrying the Bollinger in a silver bucket full of ice

*"Tonight is special Mr. Jamouri as we have a sexy fashion show hosted by a local supplier called 'Belle de Nuit' so there will be many beautiful girls here"* advised Seville.

*"I know that shop and it's owner"* revealed Mohammed turning to Jamouri and whispered,

*"He runs one of the local brothels with girls brought in from Brazil."*

The night was dark and the evening air was warm as the two henchmen sat and chatted sipping champagne observing the affluent jet-set at work enjoying themselves in this prestigious of establishments, when two stunningly beautiful young ladies, dressed in the shortest of mini-skirts and revealing practically all of their breasts, came to the table,

*"Hello gentlemen are you looking for company tonight? Would you like to give us a drink?"*

Mohammed turned to Jamouri and again whispered,

*"What do you think?"* quietly Jamouri replied,

*" No. They are the club's entertainment. Too well known!"*

Karim then spoke to the blonde girl,

*"No thankyou. Go away!"*

The girls, not used to being turned down, walked off in the hunt for some other more convivial clients to solicit.

The general overhead lights then dimmed to a low level of intensity only  to be complemented with several spotlights bathing the club in a blue hue. The loud caribbean music then lowered,

*"Senors y Senoritas, Miene Damen und Herren, Ladies and Gentlemen. Now we have the fashion show with a difference so be prepared to dig deep for these fabulous items"* came over the public address system.

Within seconds the first of the scantily clad models appeared in a shiny, black rubber one piece and started walking through the gathering, promoting the exclusive club wear from 'Belle de Nuit' only to be shortly followed by another in a pure white bra and mini dress combination. The models just kept on coming, sexily weaving their way through the audience in an attempt to promote sales.

With September being out of  high season the selection  of groups of single women was rather limited and the two Moroccan crooks were having difficulty in locating satisfactory targets to approach, however they were there for business so time was of no consequence and continued their surveillance.

Chapter 6

# _____Appointment in Banus

*"Come on Leyla the taxi will be waiting as we are five minutes late already! Have you got the money, keys, Blackberry and condoms in your bag? Come on lets go!"*

*"I am coming"* she replied  dousing herself one more time with her favourite Chanel No.5.
The look on the taxi drivers face said it all, but , what the heck this is Spain Leyla thought  quietly to herself.

*"Nikki Beach club please"* instructed Melika.

*"Si"* the grumpy driver replied.
The short drive took slightly longer than it need to as the driver could not stop peeking in his rear view mirror at the two sexily dressed girls. Being based in Marbella he was used to carrying attractive passengers but these two were exceptional to him. Each time that Melika sat forward he held the forlorn hope that at least one of her boobs might fall out. He was sadly disappointed. It came close though just as he had to turn off the N340 at Elviria!

The Seat Toledo drew up in the car park of the club where the girls jumped out, settled the fare and ran to the entrance. The noise from inside the club got them both excited to the point of them shaking their bodies in harmony to the overpowering rythm as they were ushered passed the ticket desk and into the thronging mass of beautiful, wealthy and sometimes very scantily clad women and men!

*"Oh my god Mel we have arrived right in the middle of a fashion show, fantastic."*

*"Yeah, just look at that red number there. I would like that! and that yellow leotard wow!"* Leyla remarked as she bumped into a chair by her not paying attention. Weaving their way through the heaving mass of bodies the girls eventually sighted a gap at the beach bar  so made tracks in that direction.

*"Youssef, Youssef, over there!. Do you see those two girls walking towards the bar"* Mohammed exclaimed above the din whilst grabbing Jamouri's arm and pointing at the bar.

*"Yes I see. Go, quickly and find out their situation before they get taken."*
Mohammed promptly stood up and started his assault through the crowd towards the bar taking him through the middle of the model's fashion run. At last, the Demir sisters, albeit a little exhausted from the pushing and shoving, made it to the bar,

*"What is your order girls?"* the barman shouted.

*"Erm, what shall we have Mel?"*

*"Let's make it Vodka and coke."*

*"Ok. Two vodkas and coke with plenty of ice please"* ordered Leyla.

*"Coming up"* spoke the young Spanish barman.

Within, what seemed like just a few seconds to the girls, two large tumblers half filled with vodka and ice cubes plus a couple of bottles of coke appeared in front of them,

*"That will be seventy five euros please"* the barman requested.

*"How much! Seventy five euros! No fucking way. You must be joking. We are not going to pay that! "* Leyla exclaimed.

*"You have too lady. This is Nikki Beach and you had free entry. You pay please!"* the barman demanded.

*"No way Jose are we going to pay that!"* Leyla re-stated as she was about to walk away and go back to the hotel in disgust.

*"I will pay that for them"* Mohammed intervened on hearing some of the conversation and withdrew a yellow two hundred euro note from his jacket pocket.

*"Keep the change barman for the trouble."* Immediately both the girls turned around to see who this guy was who had offered to pay for their

vodkas.

*"Hi, I'm Mohammed, please come and join me and my business partner for a drink, over there at the table"* he asked. Both girls looked at each other in the eye having cast their glance at this ethnic character with a bold tattoo on his neck. Leyla replied to the offer,

*" Can you give us a couple of minutes to think about it and thankyou for paying for our drinks?"*

*"Of course, no problem. You know where we are over there by the steps"* and walked away back to report progress to Jamouri.

*"What do you think Leyla. Shall we join them or drink up and do a runner?"*

*"He's a bit rough sis, the other looks ok and he is older. I suppose just a drink can't do any harm and afterall they have just paid for these vodkas and might come after us if we just walk out on them. Come on, we came for a good time, so let's go and have one!"*

Mohammed eventually found his way back to Jamouri who was anxious to know the outcome,

*"They are English and were about to leave as they could not afford their drinks, so those I paid for and then asked them to join us. Now they are thinking it over"* Mohammed explained

*"Well all we can do is wait. If they do not come then we will follow them into the car park"* remarked Jamouri.

Then, with a breath of enthusiasm in his voice Mohammed said,

*"Hang on I think we are in luck Youssef, they are coming over towards us.*

*"Good. They look very promising indeed"* Jamouri said as Mohammed promptly stood up to greet the approaching sisters.

*"Glad you decided to come over. Come and sit down. This is my business associate Youssef and what are your names?"*

*"I'm Leyla and this is my twin sister Melika."*

*"Are you here on holiday or do you work in Marbella?"* Youssef Jamouri asked.

In unison the girls answered

*"Holiday."*

*"On your own or with your boyfriends?"* Youssef continued.

*"No on our own. Just arrived yesterday and you, presumably you live here?"* asked Leyla.

*"No. Mohammed and I come from Morocco. I have a boat moored in Puerto Banus so we come back and forth quite regularly."*

*"That must be nice for you. I love boats. What do you do for a living?"* Melika asked.

*"I am a business man dealing in imports and exports from Morocco with Mohammed. Enough questions finish your drinks and have*

*some Champagne. Do you like Champagne?"* Jamouri asked.

*"Of course but we don't get the chance to have it very often"* replied Leyla.

*"Have as much as you like. There is plenty here"* he told them whilst reaching for the magnum bottle. It was then that Melika noticed the label,

*"Bollinger, that's a good one isn't it?"* she asked.

*"One of the best. This bottle costs two thousand euros"* Mohammed pointed out.

The talking between the four of them continued for several minutes until the announcement came over the speakers that the fashion show had finished and the main lights came on again.

At this point both Melika and Leyla agreed that they needed to visit the washroom for a brush-up so departed in the direction of the toilets.

*"What do you think Mohammed?"* Jamouri asked when the girls were safely out of earshot.

*"Perfect Youssef. They are on their own, just started the holiday so won't be missed for many days, very young and vulnerable and very, very saleable!"* Mohammed pointed out.

*"Right count them in for the first bag"* Jamouri confirmed.

Meanwhile in the toilets the twins attempted a private conversation amongst the other heavenly female bodies busily preening themselves in the mirrors.

*" Mel, what are you thoughts with these two now we have spoken with them?"* Upon hearing the conversation the girl with the long black hair standing alongside Leyla cast her eyes at Leyla's reflection. Leyla engaged the look with a brief return stare.

*"Well, as you know at the moment my boyfriend is being a prick and has been seen with another model in a bar, so why should I behave. I'm game but just for a one off as that Mohammed guy looks trouble to me. What about you?"* Mel asked. Whilst trying to apply some top-up lip gloss without being jossled by any of the other girls, Leyla replied,

*"I like that Youssef. He's quite good looking, charming, in the age group I go for and obviously rich so yes I am up for it sis."*

*"Right let's go for some fun then"* uttered Melika.

*"How about some more champagne sweethearts?"* Jamouri asked as the sisters approached the table.

*"Of course"* was Leyla's reply.
The 'getting to know each other better' conversation continued for around forty minutes whilst the Bollinger was quietly having it's effect on the young English duo. Afterall the such innocent young heads had never encountered such quality and therefore strong champagne before. A Spanish Cava or a Lambrusco would

have been the closest which they would have drunk like water. Gradually their speech was beginning to slurrrrr as Mohammed kept encouraging refills, without touching either his or Jamouri's glasses! By now Leyla's mini skirt was riding high enough for Jamouri to glance a peek at her little blue panties. He now considered this was the right time for him to bring on the final score,

*"Girls, you have both been such pleasant company I have a present for each of you"* and drew out two small boxes from the 'selection' in his inside pocket.

*"Here, these are for you."*

Gently opening the boxes each revealed an item of jewellery hidden within.

*"They are genuine antique silver lockets from my home country of Morocco"* Jamouri informed them both.

*"Oh my god thankyou Youssef"* shouted Leyla with delight and promptly leant over and kissed him on the lips followed by Melika, but with a kiss on the cheek.

*"I have one more thing to offer you"* Jamouri continued *"do you want a snort?"*

This came as a bit of a surprise to the not quite so innocent sisters from Leicester who knew exactly what he meant. Leyla, who had never been involved with the habit, turned to Melika, who had sniffed one line of coke with her boyfriend a couple of months previous ...

*"Well?"*

*"Ok just a small line  then"* Leyla replied.
     *"Very well. Come to my boat tomorrow night at around 9pm where I am having a small celebration party onboard. It's called* 
*"Ria Jocoba" and is moored in Puerto Banus in row one and we will have some fun, ok?"* invited Jamouri.
     *"Ok. We will see you tomorrow night then"* replied Leyla.
     The **Appointment in Puerto Banus** was made.

Jamouri then continued by advising that they return to their hotel to sleep off the champagne and get prepared for the late night party on the boat the following night. This the girls agreed to, gave their hosts a goodnight kiss and departed to the car park where a line of taxis were awaiting their usual custom.

## Appointment in **Puerto Banus**    *"Double Abduction"*

Chapter 7
_____**Partytime.**

The majority of the next day was spent window shopping and eating in Marbella followed by another spell of afternoon sunbathing on the beach. All the sisters could talk about was the forthcoming party on the boat and who they might meet. They were excited! and decided to go all out and dress up for the party aboard the 'Ria Jocoba' so out came the best make-up and cosmetic jewellery plus their prized silver lockets from Jamouri. Leyla plumped for her custard yellow 'Zara' mini dress with matching undies underneath and the silver heels whilst Melika preferred her more sleek black mini with red bra and knickers and the  black ' Jimmy Choo' heels. Together with the little clutch bags the twins looked stunning and were ready to go out on the pull and secretly hoping for another, possibly better, present from their host.!

  *"What time did you order the taxi for Mel?"*

 *" 9pm"*

*"Right we had better get going as it is 8.55 now"* Leyla suggested.

*"Have you got everything sis, money for the taxi, phone, keys and condoms!"* asked Melika. Quickly double checking through her clutch bag,

"yes.

Having deposited the room key at reception Leyla  could see a white taxi waiting outside so they quickly ran down the steps in the thought that it might be their's. It was.

*"Puerto Banus row 1 please"* Leyla instructed as she leant toward the driver.

*"Si chica, no problema."*

The short drive through downtown Marbella was interesting to the girls as they had not ventured that far during the day. Thus far the beach and nearby cafes and shops had been their only ports of call. Once passed the famous Marbella Beach Club Hotel,  with it's famous portico  it was only a five minute drive further along the N-340 to the marina entrance. The guard at the marina barrier stepped out of his cosy retreat to check the taxi driver's intentions,

*" Chics a el barco, Ria Jocoba en row uno"* was the responce.

*"Ah si, Senor Jamouri no problema continuar"* and signalled for the barrier to be raised.

The white Seat Toledo carefully proceeded along

the quayside with the girls sitting in awe at the designer shops, wonderful restaurants  and of course the magnificent boats gracefully bobbing up and down whilst lying at their moorings,

*"Aqui, Ria Jocoba a row uno. Viente euros par favour."*

Once Leyla's eyes had sight of the huge, imposing stern of the blue and white

"Ria Jocoba" her disbelief that this was the boat they had been invited on was all too apparant,

*"Fucking hell Mel just look at this fantastic boat. It must be worth millions! Youssef must be somebody to have a boat like this?"*

*"Christ almighty! Are we going on there and...?"* before Melika could finish her sentence who should be descending the boarding platform in the warm evening air to greet them ..... but Mohammed.

*"Salaam, good evening girls. Come aboard"* as he held out his hand to assist Leyla onto the boarding platform. Once both the girls had stepped off the platform and onto the rear teak deck Mohammed requested they remove their shoes as the heels would damage the wood decking.

*"Come inside, Mr Jamouri and his guests are waiting for you."*

Stepping through the tinted glass sedan doors into the saloon both Melika and Leyla were overcome and struck totally dumb with the opulence of the interior. The immediate adour of fresh leather purveyed the complete salon, the finish of the walnut cabinets and table was like glass and the the deep blue designer carpet, the pile of which just seemed to absorb the tanned feet of the girls, just oused total decadence and extravagence.

Breaking away from his conversation with two gentlemen dressed in the uniform of the Policia Local after handing each of them a brown envelope, Jamouri came over to greet the twins,

*"Good to see you girls. Help yourself to some Champagne and I will be with you in a minute when I have seen these gentlemen ashore."*

Having bid the police farewell he then turned to Captain Fallah, who had been sat patiently at the controls on the flying bridge waiting for instructions,

*"It's ok to start in ten minutes, captain."*

*"Very well sir, ten minutes it is."*

Jamouri re-entered the salon to attend to Melika and Leyla,

*" Sorry about that, now I can attend to you. Let's go downstairs to the lower saloon on deck two and join the other guests"* he suggested whilst putting his hands around their waists nudging them in the direction of the stairway. Still in a state of awe over the size, quality and cost of the beautiful Anaconda the sisters gingerly preceeded their host down the polished walnut stairs , along a short corridor and into the

more cosy environment of the lower windowless saloon, where they were presented by five people sitting around the semi-circular settee; Mohammed on the far left, a girl with long black hair bending forwards onto the table, next to him another good looking girl with short blonde hair next with yet another girl with red curly hair sitting beside her and finally a man, dressed in an arab djellaba, on the other end. On the surface of the walnut table lay several lines of white powder that had been carefully laid out in a series of straight, parallel lines.

*" I promised you both a snort so take a seat and help yourself,"* instructed Jamouri at which point the girl with the beautiful black hair still holding the short straw, sat up revealing her face. Leyla recognised her and the pendant around her neck at once .. it was the girl she saw in the toilet at Nikki Beach the previous night .

*"Hello, I'm Leyla and this is my sister Melika. Aren't you the girl I saw in Nikki Beach last night?"* Leyla asked.

With a slight slur in her speech the girl replied,

*"I was theeeere yes. Oh yes I remember yooooou in the mirror talking about sooooome bloke you had just met."*

*"That's right it was Mr Jamouri"* Melika interjected.

*"It's quite a coincidence that we are all here on his boat?"* remarked Leyla. Before they could talk any more Mohammed stood up and

insisted the sisters sat down and started sniffing. Leyla was beginning to feel uneasy with this situation.

*"Sit down and sniff. That's why you came"* Mohammed repeated in a raised voice. Out of a sense of fear the girls sat down and put the straws to their noses. Immediately the 'coke' hit the back of their throats  a reaction manifested. This was not standard issue found on the streets of any British town .. it was stronger, much stronger, known as 'snow'!

The man dressed in the djellaba then introduced himself,

*"I'm Mido and you are?"*

*"I'm Leyla and this is Melika."*

*"Where are you from?"* he continued.

*"England"* replied Leyla.

Jamouri had meanwhile taken up his position in an individual chair with a glass of champagne in his hand,

*"Here's to a good evening"* he toasted.Melika, who was somewhat more used to drugs than Leyla, had managed to retain some of her general awareness when she suddenly heard a rumbling coming from the rear of the boat and asked Jamouri what it was.

*" Don't worry it's only the engines. I thought we would go out of the marina and show you the nightview of Marbella from the sea"* he replied.

*"That's a nice idea"* spoke the girl with the

black hair in a voice that was becoming difficult to understand.

*" So Mido. What do you do?"* asked Melika.

*"Well, I work as an assistant in an auction house in Beni Mellal, a town in east Morocco and what about you ?"*

*"We are both fashion models in London"* Melika proudly replied.

*"Are you famous?"*

*"Not yet but we are getting there."*

Now the boat began to gently roll indicating they were out of the marina and heading out to sea.

*"Can we go upstairs and see the view then Youssef?"* asked the blonde girl who was beginning to feel  a little queasy with sea sickness.

*"Let me go and see if we are far enough out to sea first"* and promtly departed for the stairs.

Jamouri made his way to the bridge to check with Fallah and the two deckhands, Bassir and Lyam that everything was going to plan. It was. They were now some four miles out from the Spanish coast heading for the Straits of Gibraltar. Captain Fallah picked up the receiver,

*"Banus control this is M.V. "Ria Jocoba", over."*

*"'Ria Jocoba', go ahead. Over"*

*"Banus Control. Left port and returning home, out."*

*" Good night sir, out."*

Satisfied with the situation Jamouri returned to the fold in the salon and upon entering the room secretly winked his left eye at Mido, indicating that they were now clear of Spanish waters and the next stage of the plan could continue without interruption.

Standing up, Mido reached over and grabbed the hand of the black haired girl, who by now was 'well out of it' and pulled her over the table and started to drag her towards one of the cabins further down the corridor.

*"What the hell are you doing!* screamed Leyla.

*"Sit down and shut up, your turn will come"* demanded Mohammed.

*"What the fuck is going on!!"* Leyla yelled grabbing Melika's arm and started to walk to the door. Mohammed ran to catch them and threw them both back onto the settee whereupon Melika lost her balance opening her legs to reveal her red panties. It was then that Leyla, now starting to temporarily sober up as the adrenaline began pumping hard and fast around her system, caught a glimpse of the engineered grip of the revolver in Mohammed's shoulder holster which scared her. She went cold and immediately realised what was happening. All the girls, including, herself and Melika, were being kidnapped!

Both the blonde and red haired girls were almost

out cold having been subjected to the 'coke' some thirty minutes before the twins had arrived on the boat. Now was the turn of the twins to become subjected to the full power of the 'snow'.At first the ability to speak became difficult followed shortly by a semi-paralysis of the muscles. Vision was uneffected. So once fully under they could see and hear what was going on but had no ability to do anything about it.

In the cabin Mido, having thrown the girl onto the exquisitly upholstered double bed, grabbed the lapels of her blouse ripping it off with a violent yank. The same was applied to her skirt. The girl desparately tried to kick the man in his testicles but however much she tried her muscles would not allow the legs to move. Even her screaming for help became soft and incoherent. The 'snow' was in control. Soon the bra and panties had been removed from the Italian girl's body. There she lay completely naked except for her make-up and completely helpless to stop the bastard arab from starting his examination of the goods!

First the breasts, firm and natural and then the genital area to check it was shaven. It was known that the clients wanted natural, clean shaven women.

*"You will do"* then he went over to the wardrobe and removed one of the djellaba's hanging inside and slung it over the girl's back,

"Put that on when you can" and left the room, having picked up her clothes and locking the door behind him.

Bassir was conveniently on hand in the corridor to take the girls clothes from Mido for disposal later. Mido strolled back to the saloon and upon seeing him enter, Mohammed immediately grabbed the blonde haired Russian girl dragging her towards the vulgar Arab. Mido took possession and continued back down the corridor to cabin no. 2 and as before threw the girl onto the bed and continued with his examination as before.

Meanwhile back in the salon Jamouri had been eyeing up the beautiful and exposed legs belonging to Leyla. His desire for women, especially those who could not fight off his advances, was insatiable. He made his way over to the settee and sat beside Leyla's reclining body and began rubbing his hand up and down her leg. Like the other girls, Leyla was aware of what was happening but was herself now powerless to stop it. Gradually Jamouri's left hand found it's way to the yellow panties gently slipping under the delicate lace, when suddenly Mido appeared in the doorway and saw the scene,

*"Enough Youssef!, you know the terms of business with Gaber and myself, no soiled goods"* Mido forcefully pointed out.

*"Yes you are right my friend, business first but this girl is so compelling!"*

*"You must resist or buy her"* Mido stated as he now grabbed hold of the redhead, dragging her to yet another cabin. In total "Ria Jocoba"

had in excess of eight double cabins plus crew accommodation and a master suite solely for Jamouri's use.

The firey red-headed Romanian was made of stern stuff and as Mido was in the process of tearing off her dress she mustered all her available energy to shout out,

*"Qalab Wighlet haywan"* (Fuck off you animal)

which made Mido stop immediately! He then walked out of the cabin and back to see Jamouri.

*"That one, she speaks arabic so too dangerous as she could hear something and talk so she must go, now!"* he informed Jamouri.

*"Shit! Shit! we did not know that. I will get Bassir and Lyam to deal with the bitch straight away."*

*"She's in cabin 3. I will wait to check these other two girls until you are finished"* Mido advised.

Jamouri lifted the receiver from the wall bracket,

*"Fallah, send down Lyam and Bassir and tell them to bring some spare chain from the forward locker."*

It took no longer than five minutes for the two Moroccan deckhands to arrive carrying a length of chain, some twenty feet long. Without hesitation Jamouri instructed them to go to cabin 3 and dispose of the redhead.

*"Yes boss"* replied Bassir.

This was not the first time they had carried out such duties, but for the money they were being paid the two young men would ask no questions.

Their first action was to wrap the chain securely around the girl's feet then tying it off around her hands. Once completed they lifted the struggling body and carried it up to the rear deck where, without any compassion or guilt, they effortlessly threw the Romanian over the stern into the sea.

At first she floated face down on the surface of the calm sea with the "Ria Jocoba" fading away into the night, but soon the weight of the water logged clothes and the chain took hold, dragging the poor soul down into the cold depths of the Mediterranean. Down and down she drifted, with what was remaining in her mind in torment, as the light from the silvery moon grew darker and darker until it was no more. She was gone.

God rest her innocent soul.

*"All done sir "* Bassir advised Jamouri over the phone. Mido, who had meanwhile been quietly paying some attention to the two reclining sisters just realising that they were twins, instinctively knew the purpose and message from the call so was free to continue.

This time, however, he insisted Jamouri help him to drag both the girls for their examination in cabin 4, together. Taking care that no-one saw him and with a certain amount of reticence, 'The Hood,' grabbed Leyla's arms and followed on behind Mido who was likewise dragging Melika. Being one of the larger cabins, no. 4 had a king size bed allowing plenty of room for the two sisters to be thrown onto it without concern to Mido that one might fall to the floor and get injured.

*"Thankyou, Youssef you may leave the cabin now"* Mido ordered Jamouri. He wanted to carry out the examination without prying eyes, as usual, so no one could observe his actions for any later evidence or personal gain!

Apart from the occasional twitch and eyelid movement the girls lay motionless on the bed, fully aware of the activity going on around them, but powerless to present any form of defence or refusal to cooperate.

Melika's black mini dress was the first to be ripped from it's owner closely followed by the matching pillar box red bra and panties. By this time even her dignity had been removed leaving the naked, limp body available for yet another one of Mido's close examinations. The glare of horror showing on Leyla's contorted face was of no interest or concern to the bastard Mido, he just carried on regardless.

Soon Leyla's beautiful designer mini, was torn from her body, and used by Mido as a towel to wipe his hands in order to avoid any possible contamination from any of Melika's juices.Having completed and being fully satisfied with both his examinations, Mido turned both girls onto their backs, stepped back to lean against the cabin door and took time to view their beautifully formed bodies through his evil  brown, Algerian eyes. It now fully dawned on him what lay before on the bed ... a golden opportunity! But had he the guts to make use of it?

His terms of employment with Gaber's auction was ten percent commission on all sales, with the usual sale commanding around one hundred thousand dollars, returning him ten thousand per girl, but, before him lay two extremely young and stunningly beautiful twins. This was a first in his disgusting and fruitful career so could an advantage be taken, afterall, business is business he thought to himself.

As he saw it, he had the opportunity of three directions open to him. The first would be to keep the girls for himself, sell them, keep all the proceeds and disappear, the second he could demand more commission from Gaber for such a find and third do nothing and accept his usual ten percent graciously.

Should he decide on the first and Gaber caught up with him, his skin would be stripped from his body before he would be allowed to die and if he demanded more commission and Gaber refused he could see his present position being in jeopardy so maybe he should say nothing and be content with the two hundred thousand dollars he already had stashed away from several years of examinations.

Pacing up and down on the soft wall to wall carpeting within the cabin, which coincidentally was starting to sway more and more  as the "Ria Jocoba" passed through the Gibraltar straits and into the mighty swell of the Atlantic Ocean, another crazy idea flashed through Mido's mind, one that appeared pretty watertight on first imaginary calculations. During the period for the final 'preparation of the goods' in Casablanca before their onward transportation to the auction at Beni Mellal he would have a day or maybe two when he could secretly rent the sisters out to a couple of contacts from his black book for a few hours and demand a fabulous sum for the pleasure. The girls could not inform Gaber or their eventual buyers as none of them, to his knowledge, could either speak or understand English and was certain that neither of the girls could speak arabic.

There was a gentle knock on the cabin door,
*"Everything alright Mido? It's time to start the procedure."*
Mido immediately recognised  the voice to be that of Jamouri.
*"Yes. I will be ready in one minute. You can prepare the treatment but just for two!"*
*"Why only two?" Jamouri asked in surprise.*

*"I will explain soon."* Mido had made up

his mind and was mentally visualising the precautions he must now take to maintain total secrecy. No way must Gaber or Jamouri  ever find out about his anticipated actions!!

Off Jamouri walked to his suite where the 'processing kit' was locked away in a concealed compartment buried behind the headboard of the enormous bed. Once retrieved he again summoned Mohammed, Bassi and Lyam  to meet him in the salon. Eventually Mido joined the assembled group and informed them,

*"I have completed my examination of all the goods and because the last two are the first twin sisters we have ever taken they are more valuable to us all untouched. I know Gaber has a valuable client who is always on the look out for something very special and will pay heavily for it. So we only process the first two girls tonight. Youssef what is our present location?"*

*"When I last checked with Fallah we were approximately fifteen kilometres  off Tangier."*

*"Ok. Tell him to decrease speed a little as we will need a good ten hours to  prepare the goods before we reach Casablanca. Also tell him to radio Gaber to confirm our meeting for tomorrow evening at the usual place"* Mido instructed.

*"Very well"* and after handing the processing kit to Mido  he went up to the bridge.

*"Right you three follow me"* Mido commanded and led them to cabin 2 where the terrified Italian girl, having now started to come

down from the upper plane, was pressed hard against the headboard in her djellaba with a look of fear written all over her pretty face.

  *"Bassi, Lyam hold her down. Mohammed use this"* Mido commanded as he opened the small, brief case sized kit and withdrew a length of rubber piping. Mohammed was very familiar with what he had to do. Wrapping it very tightly around the girl's upper right arm her veins began to swell. Mido then withdrew the compact primus stove, placed it on the sideboard and lit the tiny wick. Having then placed the metal cup on the prongs he then tipped a minute proportion of Afganistan's best 'china white' into the cup allowing it to gently simmer, whilst emitting the faintest smell of vinegar, into a liquid before insertion into the syringe by means of the plunger. Once Mido judged the syringe to be half full and had instructed Lyam to hold her struggling arm very still he introduced the needle into the bulging vein, being certain to not miss which would result in a blister, then slowly deposited the contents into her bloodstream.
  *"Right you can all relax . We go to the other one now"* Mido commanded.

The sordid performance was then repeated on the blonde girl.
  *"We will give it around two hours before the next round"* Mido announced,

*" In the meanwhile Mohammed take the two boys to the cabin next door with the two sisters in , and check there is nothing they can use to escape with."*  This they did.

During the next couple of hours Mido and Jamouri talked in the upper salon about what extra commission might be available to them from Gaber's private sale of the twin English sisters. Not being able to come up with a definate figure Mido promised that he would carefully push Gaber as hard as possible for more money but not beyond the point which he considered that their lives might be in danger. They were both fully aware of the possible consequences of crossing or upsetting Gaber. To date they knew of at least forty-five men who did so and now eat the desert dust six feet in the ground!

*"Time for the next round of smack"* Mido interrupted,

*"go and get the boys and I will meet you in the first cabin with the black haired girl."*

Two hours with the Afgan 'snow' seeping around her system the Italian's appearance was beginning to show signs of changing. Her eyes within the blackening sockets were turning reddish with the pupils dilating and swelling bulges beneath the lower eye line were starting to manifest themselves . Her body was going limp and felt warm. For this cycle of the preparation there was still some resistance from the girl. The dependance had yet to show.

With both girls seen too, Mido decided to look in on the sisters. He entered the cabin, being careful to lock the door behind him, finding Melika and Leyla fully conscious and in a fighting mood.

Leyla was the first to speak,

*"Please, please if you let us go now we promise not to say anything, we promise!"*

*"No."*

*"What are you going to do with us?"* Melika shouted in a nervous voice?"

*"You will see!"*

*"If it's ransom, I am certain our parents will pay. Where are we going?"* Melika asked.

*"No, there is no ransom but you will never have the pleasure of seeing your parents again!"* Mido informed them at which point Leyla rushed at Mido and struck him on the face, drawing three neat lines of blood down his left cheek with her beautifully manicured nails,

*"Let us go you fucking filthy arab bastard"* and drew her hand back for another but more weighty strike. Mido was used to fiery girls and was able to strike Leyla hard across the face long before her hand could make contact with him, sending her tumbling to the floor in tears. Offering his hand to assist her back up Mido then said,

*"Look, you are both really beautiful girls and from this point your destiny has been decided. However, I am not without influence in this matter and am in a position to make your life more bearable for you both, but, you will have to look after me for me to be incentivised to look after you as best I can."* Hollow words from Mido !

*"What do you mean ?"* Melika spoke out.

*"Come over here and I will show you"* he requested.

*"Fuck off. I know exactly what you mean, pig!"* Melika replied.

*"Ok, your loss. I tried to help you"* Mido said and started towards the door.

*"Wait a minute!"* shouted Leyla as she stood up *"tell us more and maybe we might think about it."*

*"Ok. You are going to Morocco to be sold to Algerian businessmen as pleasure girls. Now it's up to me as to whether you go to a good or a bad one and believe me the bad ones are ....... well you will find out if you do not co-operate with me. When we get to Casablanca I want you to happily and willingly 'service' a friend of mine for a few hours , that's all. If everything goes to his satisfaction then I will help you to go to a good home. That's the offer, simple. Do you want to take it?"* he said with a confident smerk growing on his face.

*"What do you mean by 'service'?"* asked

Leyla.

*"Come, come. I am sure that a young girl of the world like you knows exactly what I mean, don't you!"* Mido replied.

*"You mean fuck!!"*
*"Of course .. what else" said Mido.*

Both girls starred into each others eyes with not a word being exchanged between them.

*"What choice do we have, so yes, ok, yes"* said Leyla.

*"Leyla what the fuck do you think are you saying .... no way!"* shouted Melika.

*" I will leave you to talk it over"* and Mido left the cabin, again locking it behind him.

*"Leyla we have to try and get out of this situation not accept it, so come on let's think and come up with a plan to escape!"* Melika pleaded with her calm mind.

*"Of course you are right sis, but at least let us lead the bastard on for the time being and let him think we are going to help him. It might buy us some time , so let's think. We are at sea in a boat and heading for Casablanca, wherever that is, and you cannot swim and I am not going to jump overboard and leave you behind on your own, if the chance came. We have seen at least five men aboard so it would be impossible to overcome them all and neither of us can drive a boat so escaping from the boat*

*would seem impossible. Do you agree?"*
*"Yes."*
*"So any escape will have to be made when we get to this Casablanca, agreed?"* Leyla *continued.*

*"Yes. Just had an idea. What about a message in a bottle?"* suggested Melika.
*"Good idea but we have no bottle or paper or pen Mel."*
Then an idea suddenly struck Melika,
*"Your yellow knickers. If we could write on them.... lipstick or something. Where are they?"*
*"Over there on the floor where that bastard threw them"* Leyla pointed out.
*"Now, some lipstick, lip gloss or something similar, maybe there is some in one of the drawers, let's look."*
Sure enough, as if by some act of God, following a search through the cupboards and wardrobe, there in the top drawer of one of  the built-in bedside cabinets Leyla found  a small selection of female cosmetics, jewellery and tissues etc in a small bag,
*"Here, look what I have found in this bag Mel and it's red and fuck, would you believe it, it's waterproof as well !"*
*"Ok pass me your knickers Leyla, quickly before he comes back."*
*"Mel, why not use my yellow dress instead as it is much bigger and will be seen easier in the water"* Leyla suggested.

*"True, but what if the bastard comes back for our clothes and notices it's missing? Surely there is less chance of him missing a pair of frilly knickers ..remember he is an arab !"*

*"Good thinking sis!"*
*"Let's see, I will write:*
*'HELP! KIDNAPPED! ON BOAT FOR*
*CASABLANCA FROM BANUS!"*

which Melika carefully wrote with the bright red lipstick. The wording, with a little difference in size between several of the words, just fitted onto one side of the tiny panties.

*"Ok can you open that round window Leyla."*

With the chrome wing nuts of the small porthole loosened Leyla was able the prize open the glass porthole before carefully feeding her bright yellow panties through the gap and into the warm night air where they floated gently down onto the rolling sea below to then drift on the prevailing northerly current.

*"Nothing more we can do before we get to Casablanca except pray that someone finds them Leyla."*

Chapter 8
_____ **Entry into Casablanca**


Mohammed entered through the sedan doors of the  upper salon where Jamouri and Mido were quietly conversing whilst smoking over another traditional hubble-bubble,

*"Gaber has confirmed the meeting for tomorrow at 9pm at your house, Youssef. I have informed him to expect four packages. He was not too happy with so few as he has told several of his clients there would be a choice of at least six"* Mohammed advised the two arabs.

*"Allah be with him as he will not be disappointed"* spoke Mido who rose to his feet and continued,
*"Mohammed, go and bring the two English girls here. I want Jamouri to cast his eyes on such beauty  that he has never entrapped before."*   Mido knew of Jamouri's fascination for Indian women of considerable beauty and would  relish the opportunity to gloat when seeing his frustrated associate looking at but not being able to have.

The girls heard the cabin door being unlocked and immediately on  sighting the tattooed villain strolling toward them, cowered back against the headboard in fear. Mohammed was afraid of no man or woman so the shouting and violent flapping of arms by the sisters did not present any hesitation to him . With two mighty thrusts he grabbed a hand of each girl and began to drag them into the corridor. Fearing they might be about to suffer the same fate as the other girl Leyla and Melika struggled violently to escape but to no avail as Mohammed's grip was far to powerful for either of them to overcome. Time and time again the girls bounced off the walls as they progressed down the corridor but on hitting the door of cabin 2, it opened and for a brief instant Leyla got a glimpse inside, only to see a scene she recognised, that of a person lying out cold under the effect of heroin. The open arm with a drop of blood sitting on the inner elbow joint was the final confirmation.

*"Come on you sluts get up the stairs!"*
Once in the salon both girls were paraded in their djellaba's in front of Jamouri.

*"Take off your gown's"* ordered Mido.

*"Fuck off you perverted shit"* screamed Leyla and promptly deposited a large amount of spit in his face.

Calmly wiping it from his forehead, but with embarressment in front of his colleague, Mido ordered Mohammed to forcibly strip Leyla. Taking hold of the tunic from behind he gave a tremendous downward pull tearing the cloth of Leyla's body leaving her standing completely naked in front of the now drooling Jamouri.

*"Now you will pay for that outburst. Youssef why don't you go over and touch her"* Mido suggested and ordered Mohammed to hold Leyla's arms from behind. With no more encouragement required Jamouri rushed over and placed his hands on Leyla's beating breasts. It was a gentle massage at first but soon led to a much heavier fumble. Satisfied with his effort Jamouri then lowered his hand to her groin and to insert his index finger at which point Leyla brought up her knee as hard as she could into Jamouri's well defined chin resulting in a stream of blood pouring from his broken tooth and punctured tongue.

Reeling back in pain and holding a handkerchief to his swollen mouth Jamouri disappeared down the stairs to find a washroom. Mido had had enough and could see that his intended extra remuneral arrangement in Casablanca might not happen so in a fit of rage ordered Mohammed to locate another section of chain and throw Leyla over the side.

*"No, no please you can't do that to my sister, please, please"* screamed Melika.

*"Why not?"* retorted Mido.

*"Because, because...... we will do as you want and obey your every word, won't we Leyla?"* There was a pause.

*"Yes, yes allright!"* whispered Leyla

With a look of glee in his lustful eye Mido wanted double confirmation of this promise,

*"Let's be very clear shall we. You will do anything I ask of you without question?"*
Both girls looked at each other, paused with no words spoken then turned to Mido,

*"Yes we will"* said Melika at which point the bruised Jamouri returned holding a handkerchief to his bleeding face.

*"Ok I want you to prove it. Youssef, try again but with the other girl this time"* Mido commanded.
Jamouri was only too happy to obey and headed straight over to Melika and without hesitation lifted her djellaba and inserted his finger. Melika stood motionless and expressionless whilst he finger fucked her for a second or two before he placed his swollen and bloody lips upon hers.

*"That's enough my friend. Take them back to the cabin Mohammed"* instructed Mido.

*"Enough fun for now. It must be time for another dose for the other girls so let's go and get it over with Youssef."*
With three applications to both the blonde and the Italian now complete, their 'craving for more' was just beginning to kick in. Their resistence had all but withered away, the hunger for food gone and offers of sexual favours for more supply was periodically encouraged. Mido calculated that one possibly two more doses each

would be sufficent until they reached Casablanca which the 'Ria Jocoba" should reach within a few hours time.

Fallah's radar clearly displayed the outline of the coast of Morocco and when switching to a shorter radius display the mouth of Casablanca port became visible. Picking up the receiver, Fallah spoke to Jamouri,

*" Sir. Sorry to disturb you but the port is only about one hour away now."*

*"Thankyou Captain. Advise me when we are docked"* Jamouri replied.


Dawn had come and gone by the time the Anaconda passed through the harbour mouth where Fallah pulled back on the throttles which reduced the forward speed to around three knots, this being the maximum allowed within the harbour walls,

*"Casablanca control. This is M.V. "Ria Jocoba" entering your harbour and making for Puerto de Pesca, over."*

*"Good Day captain, continue to your mooring and welcome home"* replied the port controller.

Having carefully manoeurvered the vessel through the large port to it's far end which is called   Puerto de Pesca (fishing port) Fallah prepared his mooring procedure. With Bassi on the bow and Lyam on the stern ropes, Fallah brought the "Ria Jocoba" gently alongside her usual mooring on the main pier of the fish port and as the boat fenders tenderly nudged the concrete both the deckhands lept ashore to tie off the mooring ropes. M.V. "Ria Jocoba" complete with it's crew and cargo was safely moored in Casablanca. Throttles back to neutral and the engines and electrics switched off Bassi connected the shore power supply for internal electrical operation of the boat . The sun was starting to exert it's power raising the environmental temperature up into the nineties.

Once Fallah was satisfied that all docking procedures were complete he proceeded to the lower saloon to find his boss,

*"Everything complete. We are safely moored up, sir."*

*"Ok call for the cars"* Jamouri demanded. As he reached the lower bridge to use the shore phone, Fallah observed the port customs car draw up alongside the vessel on the hardstanding.

*"Salaam"* Fallah shouted down to the uniformed officer,

*"Salaam. Is Monsieur Jamouri aboard?"* asked the officer.

*"Yes. Please come aboard and wait in the salon whilst I get him for you"* Fallah instructed. With the customs Sergeant sat comfortably on the leather sofa and a drink of juice in hand Fallah disappeared to the lower deck in pursuit of Jamouri.

*"Good morning Sergeant Bouchan. I hope everything is in order as usual?"* Jamouri addressed the officer.

*"Of course Sir, here are your completed entry papers. All I need is your usual signature."*

*"Excellent and here is your package in return, Bouchan"* handing him a sealed one inch thick brown envelope.

*"Thankyou sir. I will bid you a good day"* as he tucked the envelope into his uniform inside pocket and then off he walked down the boarding platform back to his car. Returning to the lower deck Jamouri sought out Mohammed and told him to get all the girls ready for transportation to his house as the cars would soon be arriving. Meanwhile, locked away in his private cabin, Mido had been on his mobile phone trying to contact his special friend in Casablanca to offer him the 'special arrangement' for the following day. He was lucky as Hamish, a local drug dealer who made a handsome living out of illegally exporting hashish to UK through southern Spain, was interested in hiring both the girls together as a team, for a few  hours and was willing to pay very, very well for the priviledge as long as they performed for his ritual. Whilst being nervous at the thought of hoodwinking and profiting behind Gaber's back, Mido was nevertheless content with the arrangement.

The arrangement in Casablanca
had been secured!
Jamouri knocked on Mido's cabin door,
    *"Mido the cars are here and we are about ready to depart."*
        *" Ok, I will be with you in a couple of minutes."*
Mido eventually made his way back to the upper salon and apart from Captain Fallah, Jamouri was the sole person left in the salon to direct and escort Mido to the leading Mercedes. With his fine white djellaba fluttering in the warm gentle Moroccan breeze as he walked down the platform towards terra firma, Mido insisted on checking inside the shabby Mazda mini-bus before stepping into his gleaming white limo. There inside the Mazda, once the torn curtain had been drawn to on side, he saw the four captive girls restrained by the two deckhands and Mohammed, all dressed in their robes with the hoods up. The blonde and black haired girl were so drugged they had not the slightest idea of what was happening but Leyla and Melika were far more in control, but were far too frightened to offer any resistance.
        *"Good. Keep them under control as we pass through the city, Mohammed"* instructed Mido as he slide the door closed with a loud bang before making his way to the Mercedes and jumping into the back where Jamouri was patiently waiting. The two vehicle convoy then

set off departing the Petit Port through the wrought iron gates onto the Boulevard Des Almohades, passing the old walls of the Medina, before heading up the famous Boulevard Boigny.

Chapter 9

## _____Hell in Casablanca

It was quite a task for the driver of the mini bus to keep up with the speeding Mercedes in the horrendous traffic of downtown Casablanca but he knew the directions to the house in Rue Ansari should they get parted. Rounding the rather strange hemi-spherical  metallic sculpture of the Place Des Nations Unies and onto the Ave Hassan 11 the two cars sped away in the now reducing traffic. It took several minutes driving up Hassan 11 and Boulevard Abdelmoumen at which point the Mercedes driver hung in a right turn into Rue Ahmed al Ansari and continued down for some two hundred metres. Drawing up outside the massive green gates set into the high ten foot wall of no. 68, Jamouri retrieved the remote control from the passenger locker and opened the electronic gates allowing the convoy to pass up the short drive and into the tiled, open courtyard with it's central fountain. On being certain that his gates were firmly closed and locked tight Jamouri jumped from his car and ran to the mini bus and opened the rear passenger door,

*"Ok Mohammed, you and the boys take the girls down to the cellar and make them comfortable"* he ordered.

Meanwhile Mido had been greeted at the front door by Jamouri's houseman who had further directed him into the rear garden for some refreshments. Jamouri then joined him. General conversation transpired between the two of them during which time Jamouri informed Mido about the extension and renovations he had just completed to his beautiful house which was one of the better houses in Casablanca being set in about half an acre of trees and bushes. The traditional house itself was of a modest size having only six bedrooms and four reception rooms but had the added advantage of having a double cellar which Jamouri had converted into soundproofed cells. Rue Ahmed al Ansari held a certain prestige of location within Casablanca so Jamouri's neighbours, whilst of the more affluent society, all had different ways of funding their lifestyle! Some honest but mostly ....not! This worked out well for Jamouri as everyone kept their business to themselves.

The conversation gradually diverted onto the subject of Gaber and his visit to No. 68 in a few hours time to check the packages.

*"Will you join us for dinner Mido ?"* Jamouri asked.

*"Of course I have much business to discuss with Gaber"* replied Mido.

*"Shall we go down to the cellar and see to our profit? Make sure they are well prepared for Gaber"* Jamouri suggested.

*" Good idea."*

Together they walked through one of the large reception rooms and down the stairs to the steel entrance door of the cellar. Three heavy taps on the door with Jamouri's knuckles was followed by the sound of it being unlocked from within. The door opened to reveal Mohammed standing in readiness to receive the bosses and escort them to the cells. In cell one were the blonde and black haired girls, both laid out on the wooden benches. As soon as Mido walked into the padded room the blonde, whose facial appearance had now descended to that of a street addict, sat up grabbed his hand and begged to offer him favours for a fix! Pushing her violently away Mido turned to Jamouri,

*"They are ready. Good job well done but better give them a wash and tidy up for Gaber's inspection. Now what about the English sisters let's go and have a look."*

Across the small hallway was the door to the

second cell. On entry Mido found Leyla and Melika, huddled together with their arms around each other for comfort, sitting on one of the benches. Ambling across to the cowering girls Mido seductively rubbed his filthy hands through Leyla's long auburn hair from which he felt a sense of sexual gratification. Immediately Leyla pulled back pushing his hand away. Mido leant forward and gently whispered so that neither Jamouri or Mohammed could not overhear,

*"Remember our agreement English. Do you remember?"*

With the smallest of nods Leyla acknowledged.

Stepping back into an upright stance Mido then ordered that the girls be cleaned up and properly presented to Gaber in  new and decorative djellabas. Mido was fully aware that Gaber, whom he feared when at close quarters, had been expecting more packages to auction and could possibly be in a fowl mood. If the two English girls were presented correctly then his mood could well improve.

The appointed time was approaching fast so both Jamouri and Mido took this opportunity to retire to their individual rooms for a shower and change of clothing whilst Jamouri's houseman was under instruction to liase with the cook to start preparing a good dinner of Herbal Lamb and cous-cous that he knew was to Gaber's taste.

The gold Rolex oyster strapped around Jamouri's wrist read 8:25 as he checked it whilst en-route to the main reception room.   Mido was already there, making himself at home on the pure white leather sofa sipping champagne, as Jamouri entered,

*"Come my friend Youssef, let's have a toast to a successful deal at the auction in Beni Mellal"* Mido suggested handing Jamouri a glass of his own Bollinger, which he had previously taken from the refrigerator behind the bar. On this, possibly his most fruitful trip with the taking of the English beauties, Mido cast aside his Islamic teachings and decided to partake in the infidelic habit of indulging in much alcohol!

With an intake of breath in shock, Jamouri stopped in his tracks,

*"Allah, Allah what are you doing?"*

*"Come on Youssef all rules are made to be broken we both know that don't we? A little brandy in our champagne won't do any harm "* Mido replied as he handed over the glass.

Not wishing to annoy his colleague, especially as Gaber was expected at any second, Jamouri agreed and graciously accepted the glass. Before he had time to swallow the second mouthfull in walked the houseman,

*"Excuse me sir but your guest has just arrived. His car has just entered the courtyard."*

*"Right let's go and greet him Youssef."*

The immaculate snow white Range Rover had just come to a halt as Jamouri and Mido stepped out of the villa entrance door and onto the top step. The rear door of the car opened and outstepped the familiar, imposing, but somewhat overweight, figure dressed in his usual jet black djellaba with a gold belt around his waist in which was inset a traditional curved dagger. The heavily tanned face, most of which was covered with a healthy bush of black hair, carried an evil stare. This man meant business. This was Gaber! the auctioneer who supplied the bosses of the Algerian mafia with their items of pleasure.

*"Salaam, Gaber. Your trip was good?"* Mido immediately asked walking down the steps with his arms outstretched in greeting. They kissed, cheek to cheek, in the traditional arabic way.

*"You come alone? No escort?"* Mido remarked.

*"You know very well my escort is in the crowds where no-one can see them! Besides I am returning to Beni Mellal tonight"* Gaber remarked in a tone of vulgar arrogance.

*"Jamouri, Salaam. I understand you have found me a prize catch this time?"*

*"Salaam. Yes, Gaber. Two English"* Jamouri replied. It was obvious from his muted and subdued delivery that Jamouri was acknowledging the power and control that this well-known, infamous man wealded,

*"Come into my humble home for refreshment and dinner before you set your eyes upon the catch"* Jamouri continued.

*"No, I want to see them all now!"* Gaber

insisted.

*"Very well follow me."* Jamouri led the party of three back into the house and down to the cellar. Mohammed , who had been primed to be on duty for the visit, was sitting comfortably with Lyam and Bassi in the ante room when the three burst in,

*"Mohammed, unlock the first cell"* Jamouri ordered.

Mohammed was the first to enter the darkened room, closely followed by Jamouri then Gaber and Mido.

*"These are the two normal packages, both were on their own in Marbella and will not cause any problems"* Jamouri pointed out. Again both girls offered their 'services' with outstretched hands. With his usual arrogance Gaber thrust the hands to one side. Then having given them a visual once over turned to Mido,

*"They are fine. Should bring the usual one hundred thousand dollars a piece, but did you not get three?"* Gaber asked.

*"Yes but you were told that one of them could understand arabic so I had her disposed of in the sea."*

*"Oh yes I remember, good, we do not want any risk and these they are clean"* Gaber asked further.

*"Of course, I have examined all the girls thoroughly Gaber"* Mido proudly informed him.

*"Ok time to see your special ones"* Gaber

asked.

Immediately the second cell door started to open the twins again cowered together in the far corner of their cell on Leyla's bunk.

"*So they have not been fully prepared then?*" Gaber instantly asked.

"*No. I am sure that your client, who seeks this perfection, would not want a couple of druggies!*" Mido replied.

"*You are right Mido. You are also right about their beauty.*" Gaber could not avert his eyes from gazing upon the two stunning females.

"*Out of the many years in this business I have never seen such innocent perfection Jamouri. You did well, very well*" Gaber informed him.

Turning to Mohammed, Gaber ordered him to remove their cloaks for a full appreciation of the complete package to pass across to his client. The girls struggled violently, until they saw Mido's covert gesture to co-operate, at which point they removed the cloaks themselves.

"*There have a good look you bastard*" Melika shouted as she stood up, "*Satisfied?*"

Gaber approached the naked girls, grabbed Melika on the shoulders, revealing the massive scar on his left hand received from the blow of a sword in combat, which was when she was arrested by the dramatic smell of his perfume. He then delicately slid his massive hands down Melika's arms and across to gently caress her breasts. Once the urge welled up inside him the gentleness of his touch gradually changed to a rough and rapid manilulation, to the point where it hurt Melika who responded by drawing back and whacking the arab across the face with as much force as she could muster. Gaber did not waver one ioter. His harded skin and concrete resolve could withstand a little female slap.

*"Great spirit with such exquisit beauty. You did well Jamouri. We will start at a million dollars and work down a little if necessary. Get them all ready for travel to be at Villa Dar El Hana* (which translates to serenity) *tomorrow evening. Right let's have that drink then I must return to Beni Mellal"* Gaber directed.

The three villans retired to the reception room upstairs where they partook in a glass or two of local Moroccan wine accompanied by several small bowls of black and green olives during a heart to heart business conversation. It was put forward by Gaber that the commission for the sale of the first two girls would be 10% to Jamouri and 12% to Mido but on the English twins both would receive 15% each as a bonus for securing such a prime catch. Upon hearing this offer, Mido saw red with disapproval and despite having worked with Gaber for years and fearful of his reputation was determined not to miss out on such a chance as this for just 15%,

*"No Gaber. This is a very special package and we will not settle for less than 25% each! Don't you agree Youssef?"* he argued.

*"Errrrrh yes I think 25% is reasonable"* Jamouri replied with a degree of uncertainty showing through his voice. Not often did anyone have the guts to stand against the Gaber from Beni Mellal!

Gaber was not used to having his word or propositions questioned so was direct with his reaction,
*"So you question my generousity. Without my client neither of you would get anything!"*
*"True but without the girls you would have nothing to sell!"* Mido argued.
*"Are you threatening me Mido? You work for me, remember! You would be unwise to cross me. Just think what happened to the Algerian last year!!"*
*"What did happen to him?"* Jamouri asked Mido quietly.
*"He asked for more money and ended up buried to his head in the sand when the horses rode over him afterwhich Gaber's men played polo with what remained of the head."*
*"Ok Gaber, I will settle on 20%"* stated Mido.
*"That would make you a rich man Mido, it could be as much as two hundred thousand dollars. What would you do with all that?"* Gaber remarked.
*"With an opportunity like this I would retire to my home town of Rabat."*

Gaber at once knew what course of action he would now have to take as nobody retired from his employ. He would agree terms and following the sale would arrange for Mido to disappear!

*"Very well 20% Mido and you Jamouri?"*

*"Ermmmmmm no, 15% is good enough for me"* he remarked nervously wishing to keep his head attached to his body.

*"Right, now all is agreed I will say farewell and see you all at Dar El Hana tomorrow"* and departed back to the entrance and into the waiting Range Rover which then sped off towards Marrakesh.

*"I think that went well don't you Youssef?"*

*"Yes I'm happy."*

*"Right some more wine then I think before I go back to my house for the night"* Mido suggested.

Early the following morning Mido returned in the Mercedes that Jamouri had sent across and immediately met with Jamouri for some olives and yogurt as a petit dejeuner. During the night Mido had been back in contact with his special friend, Hamish, who had agreed to visit the twins around midday at Mido's house. Once coffee had been finished Mido felt this the time to order that the twins be brought to the car,

*"Youssef, Gaber called me after he left here last night and ordered that the English twins be taken to my house for a few hours this morning as an agent of his Algerian contact would like to*

*give them a look over, so ask Mohammed to take them to the car"* was the excuse Mido gave to get the twins out of Jamouri's clutches.

*"Why can't he come here to see them?"* Jamouri asked.

*"Don't know but are you going to argue with Gaber?"*

*"No"* and requested his houseman to locate Mohammed and inform him to take the twins to the car outside in the courtyard.

———————————————

Dawn was breaking on the still Mediterranean sea as the evening's trawl was being hauled aboard the private sixty footer fishing boat 'El Barco a Mer' captained by Antonio Seville, when leading seaman Jose shouted out,

*"Que es eso?"* (What is that?) as he manhandled the boathook to pick up the object floating on the water's surface close to the net.

*"Un par de bragas amarillas!"* (A pair of yellow knickers!) he shouted in jest holding up the panties for the rest of the crew to see.

Then it became apparent to Jose that there was some writing on them, which he could not read, so proceeded to the wheelhouse where captain Seville was at the helm to see if he could translate the red script.

**"Help! Kidnapped! on boat for Casablanca from Banus"** he read out .

*"What do you think captain ...is it a joke?"* Jose asked. Despite having been floating in salt water for several hours and the aroma of fish surrounding him, when Antonio smelt the panties they seemed fresh. He could even detect a feint whiff of perfume. Seville had come to his conclusion,

*" Pull in the nets as quick as you can lads as we are heading back to Tarifa when this load is safely aboard"* he ordered. With all nets stored and all fish sorted safely away, Seville depressed the throttle to maximum and set

MFV "El Barco a Mer" on a direct heading for Tarifa in Spain.

———————————————

*"Whilst I am away better give the other girls some food and another 'shot' and I will see you back here around six"* Mido informed Jamouri and walked off to the car to await the arrival of Mohammed and the twins. Sqinting their eyes from the bright morning sunshine, Leyla and Melika, with their hands tied behind their backs, made their way down the front steps

to the open rear door of Jamouri's  Mercedes.

*"Get in there and keep quiet!"* Mohammed shouted.

*"Do you want me to come with you as security?"* Mohammed then asked Mido.

*"No. The driver and I will manage."*
No way did Mido want Jamouri's henchman anywhere near what was about to happen! Doors closed, the girls in the back and off the Mercedes sped through the gates and into Rue Ahmed Ansari where it turned left and headed for Mido's house in the village of El Gara some ten kilometres to the  east of Casablanca. The girls, terrified of not knowing exactly what was to happen to them, held each others hands tightly and desparately looked for an opportunity to escape. Their hopes were high as all they had to do, or so they thought, was to jump out of the car when it stopped in the traffic and make a run for it.
The lights in front turned red bringing the Mercedes to an abrupt halt,

*"Here's our chance Melika. Now go!"*
Leyla shouted and both girls immediately placed their backs to the doors and pulled the door handles to open the doors...., but nothing happened!. Mido turned round,

*"Did you think I would make it that easy for you. All the doors are locked"* he advised them with a smerk on his face.
Melika began to panic and started to bang the

window with her head and shouted at the drivers of the stationary traffic alongside,

*"Help, help. We need help!!!"* she screamed

*"No point in doing that as the windows are bullet proof and tinted. You can see out ok but nobody can see in!"* Mido had pleasure to inform them but still they both hit and banged at the glass. It served no useful purpose than to vent the twins frustration and desperation to escape.

The signpost indicating the entry into the village of El Gara soon came up at which point the driver swung to the left down an unmade road. The ride was uncomfortable as the Mercedes passed over one pothole after another kicking up a trail of thick dust behind as it did so. Eventually, a large set of ornate steel gates blocked the car's progress. Mido fumbled in his cloak pocket to withdraw the remote control unit. The gates casually opened, presenting a short tarmaced drive lined with tall palm trees down either side, leading up to the circular courtyard at the front of Mido's mansion.

Once again both Melika and Leyla gasped in awe at the magnitude of the lifestyle of these trafficers. They were in no doubt that they were in the hands of long established and very successful businessmen dealing in this ancient of african trades. They had been educated at their school in Leicester about the slave trade of bygone days. Little did the teachers know that it was still thriving .. but the other way round!

The car door opened allowing the girls to step out from the cool air-conditioned interior into a  wall of ferocious Moroccan heat. Now they could  fully take in the enormity of the house .. to them it was like a palace. With it's square towers topped with slatted roof's, arched windows complete with their ornately carved surroundings and the walls faced in a light brown paint, but it was the entrance that really caught the eye. The white marble steps with a delicate stream of water running down each side led up to the entrance platform on which stood two imposing marble lions, carved in a position of  readiness to pounce, fronted the main double oak doors that would not be out of place in a church.

*"Come on inside and follow me"* Mido beckoned. Through one of the oak doors, across the marble hallway, down yet another set of marble steps the  the door of a room.

*"In there, go in there and wait"* Mido ordered of the girls. So into the beautifully decorated, but windowless room, they  walked, sat down on the huge, centrally located bed and waited, not knowing for sure what was going to happen to them.

Meanwhile Mido had retired to the main reception room and poured himself a coffee whilst he waited for his friend Hamish to arrive.

The fishing vessel "El Barco a Mer" entered the mouth of the small fishing harbour at Tarifa on the incoming tide and gently cruised to it's usual mooring at the far end of the wall.

Picking up the knickers, which had been lying on the navigation table, had now dried out and Antonio was able to stuff them into his trouser pocket before jumping ashore.

*"Lads, I will be back shortly from the Capitania. Get the fish ashore and into the shed."*

It took several minutes of discussion and persuasion to convince the harbour master that the message on the panties was, in Captain Seville's opinion, true and recent and was to be acted upon. Harbour master Rodriques agreed to inform the Guardia Civil at Puerto Banus by phone.

The Station Commander at Puerto Banus, Teniente Coronel Garcia, took the call and listened intently to what the harbour master said,

*"Si Senor, repeat again please the exact words written on the knickers"* Garcia requested. Having heard the wording again Garcia responded,

*"Gracias Senor. Leave it with me"* and put down the receiver.

Fortunately the Guardia's office in Puerto Banus is in the same building as the Capitania so a meeting with the marina's Director was swift and following a brief conversation it was confirmed to Garcia that there was a vessel that left Banus a couple of days ago and was believed to be headed for Casablanca .. the vessel was called "Ria Jocoba".

*"Ria Jocoba you say!"* spoke out the man standing in the office.

*"Who are you sir?"* asked Garcia.

*"My boat was moored next to this vessel for a couple of days. Nasty looking man seemed to be the owner, an arab I think"* the man continued.

*"Interesting. Did you notice any girls or women aboard?"* asked Garcia

*"Yes I saw a couple go onboard the night it departed. Looked like they were going to a party as they were dressed up .. good looking they were!"* he informed Garcia.

*"Did the boat come back and drop the girls off, to your knowledge?"* the Coronel then asked.

*"Don't think so and I have been onboard my boat most of the time."*

Having carefully considered all the facts Coronel Garcia had a picture of events firmly established in his mind and decided to act and that speed was of the essence..

Running down to the crew room and requesting the yellow knickers be sent to him,  he then assembled the four man crew of the *Rio Arba* and prepared to start up the Rodman 55 high speed off-shore patrol boat moored on the fuel jetty. With the two diesel engines smoothly ticking over the ropes were cast off then the helmsman slammed the throttles forward for a high speed departure from Puerto Banus, creating a huge bow wave which washed up along the harbour wall, whilst Garcia plotted a course for Casablanca.

*"I want thirty five knots on a heading of 235' "* demanded Garcia of his helmsman.

Once the cruise was established he then ordered the remaining two crew to break out all the weapons and fully load them. That included the Beretta hand pistols and machine guns. Each crew member was to be issued with one of each together with fifty spare rounds. The *Rio Arba* headed through the Straits and out into the choppy Atlantic where Garcia had to reduce to twenty knots in the rougher waters.

---

The sound of the approaching car could be heard and certainly the dust cloud trailing behind could easily be seen before the hideous converted beach buggy arrived at the main gates. Hamish was arriving at Mido's house in his usual flambuoyant manner pulling up outside the house with the sound of screeching rubber. This man was a playboy, despite being in his late fifties, he was one of the richest around southern

Morocco. His highly illegal drug export business had never seen better days and anyone who was anyone in the hashish circle, from police, to customs, to port officials, was in his pocket .. a perfect contact for Mido. Mido personally greeted the ageing hippy as he tried to exit the buggy, in an elegant fashion but failing to do so,

*"Salaam Hamish. Good to see you. Come in and view the goods."*

With a porty frame clad in a loose, leather like skin and attaining around five feet four inches in height, dressed in what could only be called a suit from a charity shop, he walked up to Mido.

*"For what you asked they had better be something very special Mido!"*

*"Follow me and you will see"* Mido suggested.


Leyla, who had her ear to the door, could clearly hear the arrival of two men talking in arabic and quickly rushed back to comfort Melika who was so distressed at the thought of what she had in mind as to what was soon to happen to them both.

The door opened and in walked the familiar Mido accompanied by the rather bizarre character of Hamish.

*"There you are Hamish. Was I right to demand such a fee?"*

Hamish strolled over to the twins, who reacted by pinning themselves against the far wall. At once Mido became unsettled as he had told

Hamish they would be co-operative and attempted to coerce the girls forward, with a series of delicate hand signals, behind Hamish's back. They understood and reluctantly, very reluctantly moved forward towards the oncoming Hamish who by now had opened his mouth in anticipation revealing the three gold teeth that he had implanted to replace those he lost in an fight several years previous whilst establishing his authority within the smuggling community. Slowly circling the girls eyeing up every detail and heavily petting the buttocks to check for firmness, he returned to Mido,

*"Ok. Fifty thousand it is for two hours and anything goes, right!"* removing the wad from his inside pocket,

*"and remember I want a bowl of olives and some champagne after an hour"* Hamish demanded.

*"Of course, but I want no marks on the girls!"* Mido insisted and departed closing the door behind being certain to lock it without Hamish hearing the key turn.

Having been born on the wrong side of the street in Marrakesh, Hamish had never had the priviledge of education so could not speak English, in fact even his Arabic was that of a child's level, he therefore could not verbally communicate with the twins. But he was not there to talk! Casting off his suit and shirt he walked across to the trembling girls, grabbed

Leyla tightly and kissed her full on the mouth forcing his tongue deep, deep inside. Initially Leyla stood their rigid and drained of any emotion with this arab's tongue wandering around the inside of her mouth until Hamish lifted up her djellaba and wrapped his hand between her legs caressing her clit with his two fingers. Now she responded. Leyla was quite partial to a bit of rough handling. She put her arms around his neck and inserted her tongue deep into Hamish's mouth. Melika could not believe what she was seeing and tried to drag her sister away.

*"No Mel, we might as well enjoy it. It will be easier to accept!"* and carried on kissing Hamish at which point he then lifted Mel's cloak high above her head. Finally with some assistance from Melika the cloak fell to the floor leaving her naked. Grabbing her around the waist he pulled her towards his body and then lowered his left hand to stimulate her clit. Melika did not resist. Leyla had always had this affinity for the older man and together with the rough treatment was  being turned on. She grabbed his underpants and with a sharp jerk pulled them down allowing them to fall to the floor exposing his rather miserable excuse for an erect penis. She had seen bigger on some of the boys when she was at school! Nevertheless it was a throbbing prick so she took hold and started to caress it which had the effect of raising the arab's blood pressure to the point that he flung the two

girls onto the bed, parted Leyla's legs and pounced on her thrusting his little monster deep into her snatch whilst at the same time forcing the first three fingers of his left hand deep into Melika. Thrust after thrust after thrust Hamish pounded away, with sweat dripping from his brow, before suddenly withdrawing from Leyla only to thrust into Melika,  letting out a mighty ahhhhhhhh!!    as he did so completing his ejaculation deep within, taking both the girls completely by surprise with his lack of control. Melika then vomited.

Normally after such action most men would fall back and relax but this tenacious little arab was determined to get his monies worth and took hold of the girl's heads and pulled them both down onto his now damp and rapidly deminishing penis and held them there. He wanted it brought back to life as soon as nature would allow. With such attention from two such beautiful young white girls with their tongues slipping up and down the shaft, Hamish's penis was given no chance to relax and within seconds was again as straight as a pygmy's arrow. This time Hamish wanted to explore the pleasure, forbidden by Muslim women, that of anal penetration. Never would he be able to repeat this opportunity so now was the time for him to take full advantage, and experience the forbidden excitement of anal pleasure, he thought. It took several minutes of attentive oral care from Leyla and Melika for the Moroccan to be confident of a sufficiently hard penis for his first attempt at anal entry. He selected Leyla for the priviledge so stood up turned her over, in a rough manner, onto her chest before drawing up her backside and parting her legs in preparation for his entry. Upon realising what this bastard was about to do to her sister and probably to her afterwards Melika went puce in the face with anger, so carefully manoeuvred herself behind Hamish, clinching her fists tightly in readiness to strike the invading arab on the back of his neck. She  raised her arms high above her head in readiness to strike at exactly the point when the bastard was about to enter Leyla. Push and in he went with Leyla emitting an almighty scream from the intense pain. Despite the compactness of his manhood Leyla's virgin anus had great difficulty in accepting it. Melika's arms trembled and her upper arm muscles contracted gathering strength with which to bear down on the perspiring neck ... but she froze. Melika could not forget what Mido had said to her and even if she stopped the rape what would happen to them both then. It could only get worse . So she drew back, relaxed her muscles and watched as her sister was being brutally abused whilst pissing herself that her turn would undoubtly be coming soon.

Tears of despair began  gently rolling down her cheeks. Leyla's screams got louder and louder the more the Moroccan bastard thrusted. The pain for Leyla became excrushiating to the point when he dug his fingernails into her ribs for a firmer grip she passed out collapsing onto the bed, but still the bastard continued on thrusting away. Melika was  going out of her mind with hopeless frustration, her vision became obscured with the tears and her head was swimming with anger, when suddenly, out of the corner of her left eye, she caught a blurred glimpse of a shiny object protruding from the arab's jacket lying  on the floor. Somehow, she knew not from where, she instinctively realised what it was and in the uncontrollable passion of the moment bent down, pulled the knife from it's sheaf in the inside pocket, raised it high above her head with both hands firmly wrapped around the short handle and with all her might brought it hard down into the back of the Moroccan's neck burying the blade deep into the flesh up to it's hilt. Hamish instantly reeled backwards in pain and shock and was dead before he hit the floor.. With  blood still dripping from her hands Melika bent over the unconscious body of  her dear, dear sister and attempted to clear away some of the  blood that was gently weeping from her torn anus before turning her  over and comforting her as Leyla began to come around.

*"Leyla, Leyla come on wake up we have a problem to talk through, come on wake up"* Melika kept repeating. Eventually Leyla came round with her first reaction being that of comforting her rear which had become so sore. Once totally back in the land of reality, it was

then that Leyla noticed the naked body lying on the floor in a pool of blood.

*"What the fuck happened. Is he dead?"* she shouted.

*"Yes I killed him"* Melika informed her.

*"Fucking hell sis that means that bastard upstairs will kill us for this. What have you done! Let's try the door and see if we can get out of here"* Leyla suggested. The pain was almost too much for her to bear finding it almost impossible to walk, but she made it only to find it locked.

*"Fuck, fuck. What the hell are we going to do now!!"*

Trying to put the emotion of the moment to one side and think quickly Melika slowly and with a certain amount of reluctance, leant down and withdrew the knife from Hamish's neck,

*"Leyla go back and lay on the bed and rest till someone comes in, whilst I will wait behind the door ready to kill whoever comes in. Then we try to escape through the house. It's our only chance, meanwhile try and push the body under the bed out of sight"* Melika commanded as she attemped to take advantage of the situation they now found themselves in.

*"Good idea sis"* and walked over to move the body of the fowl arab. Despite his petite statue, the dead weight of the Moroccan's body proved hard for Leyla to shift, but she gave it her all, casting her pain aside. The polished marble floor did help, however the act of touching a dead

body, especially a naked one, filled her with revulsion but she continued managing to secrete it up to the lower torso underneath before they both heard the knock on the door followed by the turning of the key.

*"It's only me Hamish with the champagne."*

Immediately Melika leant back hard against the wall, knife in her right hand held high above her head in readiness to  strike the intruder. The door opened and in walked Mido who immediately saw the remains of the  protruding body from under the bed which only had one of the girls upon it and instinctively, in the flicker of an eyelid, put two and two together, swung around raising his free arm as protection against the oncoming knife held so firmly in Melika's hand as it bore down upon him. The thin blade entered through the bandage covering the previous wound, of his lower left forearm, allowing Mido's right fist to come sharply around and make contact with Melika's cheek sending her to the floor.

Withdrawing the knife from his arm, for the second time, proved painful but not life threatening to Mido,

*"What have you done you assholes"* he shouted departing the room whilst clutching his arm in pain before locking the door behind.

*Chapter 10*

_____**The Auction Approaches**

Twenty or so agonising minutes later, after having come to the conclusion to hastily arrange with his houseman to bury the body in the garden to a depth of at least three metres to avoid detection then to drive the beach buggy to a public car park in Marrakesh whilst dressed in Hamish's clothes only to abandon it there and further calculating that Hamish would probably not have told any of his household where he was going. He gambled that no-one would connect him with Hamish's eventual disappearance. Mido returned, with his arm in a new bandage, to the downstairs room.

By now both girls had replaced their djellaba's and waited in fear for their lives as Mido walked in,

*"That was a stupid and potentially dangerous thing you did! Hamish is one of the baddest men around. All our lives are now in danger. We will   continue to meet up with Gaber and you will say nothing about what happened. If you do I will kill you both. Do you understand!!"*

Without hesitation both girls agreed.

*" Right you will both follow me back to the car and remember you will say nothing to the driver, nothing. Do you understand, nothing"* Mido commanded.

---

*"Casablanca control. This is Coronel Garcia of the  Guadia aboard vessel Rio Arba, Do you read, over"* spoke Coronel Garcia.

*"This is Casablanca control., go ahead Sir."*

*"We are here on official business. Permission to moor, over?."*

*"Permission granted Sir."*

The Rodman pulled up alongside the Harbour Office with Garcia jumping ashore before the ropes were secure and quickly made his way up the stairs to the Harbour Office where he burst in through the door,

*" Who is the senior officer on duty?"* he requested.

*"Salaam. That's me Coronel. I'm Harbour Master Mustafa. How can I help you?"*

*"Do you have a vessel moored here called Ria Jocoba?"* Garcia asked.

Mustafa took the log from the desk and ran his finger down the entries,

*"Ah yes Ria Jocoba. She came in yesterday morning and moored in the fishing section."*

*"Do you know the owner?"* Garcia

continued.

*"Youssef Jamouri"* replied Mustafa.

*"Can you get me the Chief of Police or Customs"* the Coronel then asked.

*"We only have Sergeant Bouchan on duty today and he is downstairs in Immigration/ Customs"* responded Mustafa.

*"Tell him to come here pronto"* Garcia ordered before realising that his authority in Morocco was severely limited although relations between Spain and Morocco were very close.

Within five minutes the heavy steps of Bouchan could be heard coming up the steps. The door opened,

*"Who wants to see me?"* he asked.

*"This is Coronel Garcia from Marbella Guadia Civil. He wants to ask you about vessel Ria Jocoba"* Mustafa advised him at which point Bouchan became nervous and started to form beadetts of sweat on his forehead.

*"Sergeant, do you know vessel Ria Jocoba and it's owner?"* Garcia asked.

*"Yes sir, I saw Mr Jamouri yesterday on board the boat"* the nervous Bouchan replied.

*" Did you see any women aboard?"*

*"No."*

*"Did you check through the boat?"*

There was a prolonged silence before Sergeant Bouchan gathered his thoughts to reply,

*" Errrh , no sir."*

*"You are familiar with the owner?"* Mustafa then asked as he, like Garcia, began to

smell corruption at work.

*"Yes. I check him in several times a year but there is never a problem!"* Bouchan stated.

*"Mustafa will you contact your local Surete National Guard commander and tell him to bring four men  and a vehicle or vehicles to carry eight, here immediately"* Garcia ordered.

———————————————

Once again the white Mercedes pulled up outside the gates of no. 68 where the driver used the remote control. Inside Jamouri was anxiously pacing up and down the courtyard awaiting the return of Mido and the girls and was so relieved when he saw his car drive in,

*"Good to see you back Mido. Everything go ok. Did the Algerian agent turn up?"* Jamouri asked.

Knowing that Jamouri's driver had seen the buggy with Hamish at the wheel arrive at his house, Mido thought it best to admit the agent had arrived but left after him.

*"We must be off to Beni Mellal within half an hour"* Mido confirmed.

*"Are the other girls ready to travel?"* Mido then asked.

*"Yes, Mohammed is bringing  them  up to the mini-bus as we speak"* Jamouri replied.

*"Good, so these two English girls can transfer to the mini bus now"* as he opened the rear door of the Mercedes. As Melika stepped out

Jamouri caught a glimpse of her face which had now developed a large purple bruise on one side.

*"What the hell happened to this one Mido!"* he then asked.

*"A slight problem with manners, but all is ok now"* Mido responded.

*"What will Gaber think?"* asked Jamouri.

*"Who cares what he thinks!"* exclaimed Mido in a defiant mood of nervous anguish.

The other girls appeared in the doorway with Mohammed who escorted them across to the courtyard and into the bus, where they were bundled into the rear to join the waiting twins together with Lyam and Bassi.

Everything was set for the three hour journey to Beni Mellal.

After a final check round of the house and a few brief words with his houseman Jamouri jumped into the rear of the white Mercedes to join Mido and gave instructions to the driver to proceed. Back down the short drive, out through the gates and onto Rue Ansari heading south east to pick up the N11 autoroute the two vehicles sped away in convoy.

---

Garcia could clearly see the oncoming jeeps so following behind Bouchan he descended the steps to greet the two jeep convoy as it drew up outside the Harbour Office. As the front M151 jeep came to it's abrupt halt out stepped the

Moroccan commander in his smart black, well pressed uniform,

*"Salaam, you must be Coronel Garcia sir"* and promptly came to the salute,

*"I am Lieutenant Asan of the Surete Nationale de Casablanca. How can we help you sir?"*

*"I want you to take me, my men and Sergeant Bouchan to the vessel Ria Jocoba moored in the fishing dock where we will be searching it and I am expecting possible resistance, Lieutenant"* commanded Garcia.

*"Very well sir. What will we be searching for?"*

*"Female slaves abducted from Spain"* replied Garcia. On overhearing this reply to the Lieutenant, Sergeant Bouchan suddenly felt a cold shiver run down the length of his back once again. He had been taking financial reward for several years from Jamouri to sign off the customs declaration on the re-entry of his boat into Casablanca, but never realised that a cargo of slaves was onboard each time. If his connection with Jamouri was ever established then he would most certainly be executed.

With everyone aboard the M151's and all weapons checked, off the soldiers sped to challenge the Ria Jocoba.

With the beautiful blue hulled boat in sight the driver of the lead jeep increased speed to lessen the chance of too much notice been given to those who might be onboard. In a cloud of dust the two jeeps pulled up hard to a crescendo of screeching rubber before the soldiers lept to the ground and took up positions on the hardstanding alongside the Ria Jocoba with their MAC1950 assault rifles and Beretta's in a firing position, ready for any defense. They was no sign of life aboard showing from the shore, until Garcia suddenly caught sight of the wavering of one of the curtains in the upper salon.

Immediately Garcia shouted out,

*"Ria Jocoba, who ever is aboard come out with your hands in the air! Now!"*

Silence! Not a sound to be heard.

*"Very well we are coming aboard"* shouted Garcia and started towards the gangway followed by Asan and Bouchan, all with pistols in hand. When Garcia was around half-way across, the sedan doors of the upper saloon opened and out stepped Captain Fallah,

*"Salaam gentlemen. How can I help you?"* he asked.

*"Who is onboard?"* asked the Lieutenant.

*"Only me."*

*"Where is the owner, Mr Jamouri?"* asked Garcia.

*"I cannot tell you that. Hello Sergeant Bouchan. What's this all about?"* replied Fallah.

*"We are going to search the boat"* advised Lieutenant Asan who then signalled for the soldiers to come aboard.

*"Captain , I will ask you nicely only once more. Where is the owner?"* Garcia demanded.

For fear of his life if he talked Fallah refused to co-operate and sat down and said nothing.

*"Very well. Lieutenant instruct your men to take the boat apart please. I and my men will stay her with Bouchan and the captain"* the Coronel ordered.

The next ten or so minutes passed slowly, with Bouchan becoming more and more nervous and frightened, when one of the soldiers came up the stairs carrying a bundle of female clothing.

*"We found these hidden in one of the cabins sir "* handing them to Garcia. In the bundle was a yellow dress, a black dress, a pair of matching red undies and a yellow bra. Instantly Coronel Garcia put his left hand in his pocket and withdrew the pair of yellow knickers that the fishermen had pulled out of the sea and compared it's lable with that on the yellow bra .. they were identical .. conclusive prove that the kidnap story was true and that the kidnapped girl had been on 'Ria Jocoba.' Turning to Asan Garcia ordered,

*"Lieutenant. I want you to arrest the captain, now!"* at which point Fallah lost his composure and suggested Garcia ask Bouchan for Jamouri's whereabouts. Bouchan panicked and made a run for the back deck where he jumped into the water to try and make a break for it. Out of trained impulse one of Asan's men raised his rifle and pulled the trigger hitting Bouchan in the back of the head ....... he was

dead.

"*Get him out of the water*" ordered Asan. Now the full attention of both Coronel and Lieutenant was directed toward Fallah.

"*Right you have precisely ten seconds to tell me where Jamouri lives!*" Asan informed him. The saloon fell silent,

"*9, 8, 7, 6, 5, 4, 3, 2, 1.*" Asan counted down ...nothing not a word from Fallah.

"*Ok. We will do it the hard way*" then turning to two of his men Asan ordered them to hold out Fallah's hand flat on the table. Asan then removed his pistol from it's holster, grasped it by the barrel and raised it to head height.

"*One more time. Where does the owner live?*"

Silence ...... then with all his force the Lieutenant smashed the butt of the pistol onto Fallah's fingers. The yelp of pain could be heard on the other side of the port!

"*I ask you again captain?*"

Again no response, so this time Asan took the pistol by it's butt, pointed the barrel at Fallah's left foot and put a round through it. By now a copius amount of blood was soaking into a large area of the beautiful carpet.

Fallah was reeling on the floor in excruciating pain

"*Just one more time captain. Where does he live?*" Asan repeated as he placed the barrel into Fallah's mouth and cocked it. Fallah could see the pressure of Asan's finger increase on the trigger,

*"Ok I will tell you. It's 68 Rue Ansari"* and then promtly passed out with the pain.

*"Handcuff him to the table"* Asan ordered *"and then all of us get back to the jeeps."*

Speeding through the streets of Casablanca the two jeep convoy soon reached Rue Ahmed El Ansari where it pulled up outside the gates of No. 68. Outstepped the Surete Lieutenant who walked to the door bell and pressed it.

*"Yes"* came through the intercom.

*"This is the Surete Nationale will you open the gates please"* ordered Asan.

A minute or two passed before the buzz of the unlocking gate mechanism could be heard, allowing Jamouri's housekeeper to compose his thoughts and grap hold of a pistol from his room which he then tucked away under his cloak. The gates opened and in stormed the two M151's. The soldiers rapidly dispersed around the front of the house taking up their now familiar firing stance. The two officers ran up to the front door only to find it closed and locked.

*"Open up in the name of the Surete"* shouted Asan as he repeatedly banged on the door with the butt of his Beretta pistol. The key turned and as the door started to move open Asan put his shoulder hard into it forcing the door open fast which had the added benefit of knocking the houseman to the floor so when Asan entered he had control of the situation at pistol point.

*"Is Jamouri in?"* asked Asan.

*"No sir. He has gone"* replied the frightened houseman.

*"Where has he gone to?"* demanded Garcia.

*"I cannot tell you as I don't know."*

*"I don't believe you. Now where is he?"* ordered Asan.

*"I cannot tell you sir!!"*

At this point the Lieutenant signalled for both his and Garcia's men to carry out a full search of the house whilst he continued questioning the houseman. It was not long before one of the Surete soldiers beckoned his commander to come and view one of the rooms in the basement. On entering the padded room, both officers were appalled at what they saw: a crumpled double bed with a substantial amount of blood on the sheets, a length of rubber tubing on one of the sidetables but worse of all on the other sidetable was a collection of syringes, a couple of blackened spoons, a small quantity of Afganistan's best and a cigarette lighter. It was more than obvious to the officers what had been going on here.

*"Oh my God, may Allah be forgiven, this, this obsenity in my country and in my town, I'm ashamed Coronel. We must wipe these bastards out"* Asan uttered.

Following an 'in-depth' search of the entire house where no corner was left untouched, the entire business that Jamouri had been involved in became exposed, except for one thing, the location of the sales exchange point for the girls. Apart from the houseman, who might have some knowledge, there were no further leads to follow.

*"Ok, go and get the houseman down here "* Asan demanded of his soldiers.

With his arms held firmly behind his back the houseman was forcible pushed into the room and manhandled onto the one and only chair. His hands were secured to the chair with rope.

*"Now where is Jamouri?"* the Lieutenant demanded.

*"I cannot tell you, my family you understand sir"* the man replied.

*"We are not interested in you or your family. Where is Jamouri. I will give you to 10! We have killed one of your colleagues already. Another won't matter"* Asan informed him.

*"8, 7, 6, 5, 4, 3, 2, 1"* he counted down. Nothing the man said nothing.

*"Very well. Private Hassan work him over"* ordered Asan as he stepped out of the way to allow Hassan some space.

Thack! Thack! Thack! as the hugely built private hit the houseman in the face six times with his clenched fists drawing blood to flow from his mouth and a couple of teeth to fall to the floor. Even Hassan's knuckles had become severely bruised.

Lieutenant Asan intervened,

*"Enough private. Ok where is Jamouri?"*
*"I do not know!!"*

*"Very well. Private Hassan, remove his shoes and use your rifle."*

Hassan complied and raised the upright assault rifle to bring the butt down heavily on the houseman's left foot. The yelling of pain could be heard throughout the house, possibly even the whole of Casablanca!.

Again Asan asked,

*"Where is Jamouri?"*

*"Sir I cannot, my wife and child!"*

*"The other foot private."*

Again the screams of pain were intolerable for the man. At his point Garcia spoke out,

*"Your methods are very violent Lieutenant!"*

*"In Morocco sir, we treat criminals as dogshit!"* Asan replied.

Then turning back to the houseman,

*"Now one more time where is Jamouri?"*

*"My wife sir, my wife!!"* he pleaded.

*"I am losing patience with you. Private , now the knees!"*

As Hassan raised the rifle, tightened his arm muscles and started the descent......

*"Ok Ok Ok!!. No more please no more!! He went with Mido in the Mercedes to Beni Mellal to see a man with a white 4x4. I swear that's all I know. I swear sir."* Hassan halted his action.

*"Where in Beni Mellal and what man?"*

*"I swear I do not know. They went about an hour ago to sell the girls that's all they told*

*me."*

*"What is the registration of the Mercedes?"* Asan then asked.

*"I do not know. Its white with black glass. That's everything sirrrrrrrrr."* His body went limp, his head fell forward as the houseman passed out with the pain.

*"How far is this Beni place and is it big city or small town ?"* Garcia asked.

*"About two hours drive south east from here and it's a lot smaller than Casablanca"* Asan advised him.

*"Then let's go there and see if we can find the car. With only an hour's start we might hit lucky"* ordered Garcia. So off they all ran back to the jeeps, leaving the houseman bound to the chair and headed  for Beni Mellal with as much speed as the traffic would allow.

———————————

Having driven across the baking hot, fertile plain and through countless olive and orange groves at a steady forty kilometres per hour, which was just about as fast as the old Mazda mini-bus could muster, the convoy of the white Mercedes and Mazda entered the periphery of the modern town of Beni Mellal only to get caught up in the traffic of Boulevard Mohammed V reducing their speed to a walking pace at which point Mohammed double checked that the curtains shielded the girls from public view.

Meanwhile the Lieutenant's jeeps, which had been able to maintain a much higher average speed of ninety kilometres per hour  from Casablanca, had also just entered Beni Mellal and without realising it were only just a few cars behind the mini-bus.

*"Why are there so many goddam white Mercedes cars in Morocco ?"* asked Garcia.

*"Good car. Last's a long time Coronel"* Asan remarked.

*"How the hell are we going to find Jamouri's in this lot?"*

*"Remember he has black glass"* the Moroccan reminded Garcia then continued,

*"I suggest we cruise the length of Mohammed V and if we have no sighting then we go to the Police Nationale station and seek their help as well."*

Having crept passed the Post Principale (post office) Jamouri's driver indicated for a left turn into Bd de l'Armee Royale where he would head up the hill towards the  Mosque. Gaber's house was within sight of this old and beautiful Mosque. The turning arrived with both the Mercedes and Mazda mini-bus being then able to increase speed. As the diesel fuel lorry travelling immediately behind the mini-bus also turned into l'Armee Royale it shielded the view of the rear of the Mazda from Garcia's beedy eyes as the Surete convoy continued straight on up

Mohammed V. They had been no more that fifty metres from the girls but had no idea!

With the Mosque in sight the driver knew, from his many visits, to indicate right and turn alongside the ancient building into Rue Marmais. At the far end, as the road ran out into a sandy track but still under the eaves of the great building, there stood a set of very ornate and solidly constructed steel gates. The convoy halted whilst the driver alighted from the Mercedes to press the entry button to Villa Dar El Hana. This was Gaber's house.

The property was extensive and totally surrounded by a two metre high hardened mud wall with castellations. Gaber was a private man and loved his own, plus the ocassional woman's, company. The Hugh Hefner of Beni Mellal. His living was made from the regular trafficking of abducted females to the  bosses of the Algeria mafia, of which there were many. His business was secure and without risk, as by design, all his clients came from across the Algerian border and more importantly they were the  mafia bosses of the local provinces. Following their purchases at his auction they would all to a man return with their girls back to Algeria where very few white westerners venture and none were certain to follow on any rescue attempts.

The convoy drew up alongside Gaber's white Range Rover. Jamouri and Mido stepped outside onto the compacted sandy drive and made their way to the imposing entrance vestible of the massive, white painted house. Before either of them could reach for the wrought iron door pull, the main oak door opened to reveal the smartly dressed houseman waiting to welcome them in,

*"Salaam gentlemen, Monsieur Gaber is waiting for you in the main saloon. Follow me please."*

Both men had visited Gaber's house on several occasions so were very familiar with the extended directions through the never ending plethora of corridors to the lavish saloon with it's adjoining garden conservatory where Gaber sat enjoying his afternoon puff on his hubble bubble,

*"Salaam gentlemen. Come and share a smoke with me  before we depart for the fort. I take it the girls are well looked after in the transport? "* Gaber inquired.

*"But of course"* retorted Mido in an indignant tone. All three observed the customary smoke and idle chit-chat before Gaber stood up, shook down his black djellaba, adjusted the angle of his dagger and walked towards the door,

*"Gentlemen. We go to the fort and make final preparations for tonight."*

Gaber, escorted by his houseman and a couple of security men, led the convoy in his Range Rover closely followed by Jamouri in the Merc with the mini bus trailing behind, as they set off down the drive and out through the main gates on to Rue Marmais. Destination :

The fortress of Tadla.

Having traversed the full length of Mohammed V

several times and not spotting a Mercedes with darkened windows, Lieutenant Asan decided that now was the time to call into the Beni branch of the Surete and seek assistance so diverted the two jeep convoy into  Bd de 2 Mars where he knew the Surete outpost was located. Following a rather protracted conversation with the local Commander of Post it was rapidly established that a well known character of a dubious reputation, who owned a white Range Rover, lived in Beni Mellal .. his name Mohammed Gaber.

Immediately The lieutenant instructed the commander to assemble a force to join himself and Garcia for an assault on Gaber's house. Within the hour the combined strength of twenty or so troops were congregated at the gates to Gaber's house.

*"Commander, I want you and your force to enter from the rear of the property when I blow these gates to cut off any retreating people. Take them alive if possible and be careful not to shoot any females as they maybe some of the prisoners"* ordered Asan.

The local force scattered around the castellated walls to the far side of Gaber's property and prepared to scale the wall with their grappling lines. Meanwhile Asan had hung a series of small charges on the main gate hinges and ordered everyone to stand back and await the detonation .......... BANG! Off it went with the gates falling to the ground in a huge cloud of sanddust. Before it could settle the combined force of Surete and Guardia charged into the grounds, spreading out, with guns at the ready, as they rushed towards the house. At the rear, the local Surete had scaled the walls and were closing in to the rear entrance to the house through the extensive gardens and fountains.

Silence... dead silence. The house was surrounded by the combined forces .. there had been no resistance. The Moroccan lieutenant turned to the Spanish Coronel,

*"I do not like this Coronel, either the house is empty or they saw us coming and are waiting inside for us to enter!"*

*"We have no choice but to enter Asan ..let's go!"* Garcia shouted as now, like everyone else, the adrenaline was pumping and courage was running high.

Several smoke grenades were thrown through the front windows consecutively as the front door was blown wide open .. meanwhile the rear guard heard the explosions and gained their entry through the rear french doors. Every room in the house was checked, commando style with guns ready to fire if encountering opposition. No-one. The house was deserted.

*"Shit, shit looks like we might be too late!"* shouted Garcia.

*"Let's not give up yet"* as Asan instructed his men to search for some form of clue or evidence that might help to locate the girls. Some forty or so minutes past before the senior NCO

reported back to Lieutenant Asan,

*"Sir, we have been through everything. The house is clean..there is nothing, absolutely nothing here that can help us."*

Whilst pacing up and down the saloon in thought, Asan suddenly looked up at the picture mounted above the exquisit bureau and something registered in his brain. It was a magnificent watercolour of the Fortress at Tadla.

*"Tadla! The Fortress. Of course the perfect remote place for storage and auction of illegal merchandice."*

*"What is Tadla?"* asked Garcia.

*"It's an ancient 17th century castle built by Sultan Ismail sited on the foothills of Mount Tassemit overlooking Beni Mellal .. come outside Coronel I will show you"* Asan suggested.

Once outside in the courtyard Asan pointed towards the eastern hills (Atlas Mountains) and there, perched on a plateau of solid rock half way up the mountain isolated from the world, was an ancient fortification consisting of four large towers bordering a square building

... the Fortress of Tadla.

*"Ok there's nothing else to go on so let's give it a try "* said Garcia.

With all the men re-assembled aboard the jeeps and with Asan leading, the convoy set off for the Fortress.

Having safely negotiated the afternoon traffic and traversed the extensive olive groves en-route to the foothills of the Atlas Mountains Gaber, with his collection of vehicles, sped through the twin towers guarding the entrance to the fortress in a cloud of orange coloured dust before sliding to a halt at the site of the original drawbridge, now replaced by a strong oak walkway.

It was quite a team that crossed the walkway: Gaber, Mido, Jamouri, Mohammed, Bassir, Lyam, security and of course the four girls looking all looking tired and the worse for wear , still held together with a rope. Both Jamouri's and Gaber's drivers remained with the cars.

Melika tried hard to slow the party down by grabbing the handrail but Mohammed was having none of it and kept pulling her away. The black haired girl fell to the ground being so weak from a lack of proper food. Lyam and Bassir were quick to pick her up and take her by the arms.

Once over the bridge and standing in front of the massive three hundred and fifty year old arched, entrance doors, Gaber ordered that all four girls be taken to the holding pens in the lower cellars whilst he, Mido and Jamouri would make their way to the 'auction' room on the top floor of one of the four huge square towers.

 Having over the years become one of the major

dignitaries of Beni Mellal, Gaber had been elected 'Keeper of the Fortress' which allowed him to have the sole set of keys to the main doors and further had the final say in who and when anyone could use the facility. It was the perfect set up for Gaber's illicit activities.

The Italian and Russian girls were not in a state of mind to fully take in what was happening or where they were, but Melika and Leyla were. All the time looking for a means of escape but in this dark, stone, underground environment neither could come up with any ideas. On reaching the lower section of steps it became apparant to Melika that there were other girls here . The occasional moan could clearly be heard from inside one of the many rooms.

*"In here. You go in here!"* ordered Mohammed as he open the wooden door to expose a small windowless room containing three other girls lying on makeshift beds. All drugged to the eyeballs like the Italian and Russian .

*"Time for one more shot for these two before the guests arrive"* suggested Mohammed as he unwrapped his injection kit and bound the girls arms. The door slammed shut as the Moroccans left the room leaving it in complete darkness. Leyla clutched her sister close,

*"Christ I'm scarred Mel. Hold me tight. How the fuck are we going to get out of this!"*

*"I've no idea but we must hold on. Something will present itself. Maybe we kneel*

*down and pray?"* Melika uttered.

*"Does anyone here speak english?"* she asked out loudly. Silence! Either no-one understood or they were all so drugged they could not respond. So both sisters fell to their knees and cupped their hands in silent prayer for some divine help.

Mohammed and the two crewhands made their way to one of the rooms on the first floor where they joined several other rough looking Moroccan men who had previously delivered the other nine girls abducted from various seaside resorts in Portugal and France.

Meanwhile, up in the huge 'auction room' Gaber was starting to re-arrange the stageing, chairs and tables into an informal auction format in readiness for the Algerian bidders arrival later on that evening.

---

It was as the lead jeep left the outermost dwelling of Beni and could just see the fortress towers in the long distance that Lieutenant Asan suddenly thought better of their strategic situation and suggested to Garcia that they return to Surete HQ for further soldiers and arms. It was begining to dawn on Asan that the auction, if it were to be imminent, could involve a great deal of rather ugly and dangerous thugs who undoubtedly would be well armed and escorted by further armed bodyguards. Garcia agreed. The mini convoy of M151's turned about and rapidly headed back to Bd de 2 Mars.

Pulling up outside the rather plain building Asan lept from the lead jeep, ran up the steps into the main reception area and ordered the desk Sergeant to call in as many able bodied soldiers as he could including those on leave or off-duty. Meanwhile, the Armoury NCO was summoned and ordered to break-out the Russian AK-47 assault rifles plus fifty rounds each and pistols for immediate distribution to all soldiers. During this period whilst the force was being established and equipped Asan and Garcia patiently waited, taking advantage of this time to request a survey map of the Fortress at Tadla from the local Qadawat (Rural District Council) to help construct an attack strategy for when they eventually arrived at the fortress.

———————————————

Gaber took up a stance on the makeshift stage, surveyed the rather stark room ensuring that he would be able to see all bids even if they were at the very back of the room and having being satisfied with his elevation suggested Mido and Jamouri escort him down to check that the women were all cleaned up for best presentation to the audience. Entering the first cell allowing the hallway light to penetrate and illuminate the crouching girls, it was immediately obvious to Gaber that they were in need of a facial wash,

*"Jamouri. Instruct Mohammed to arrange*

*all the girls faces to be washed and their hair to be tied back and then spray them all with some sort of Sandalwood perfume. After all they must be appealling to fetch the highest price for us"* said Gaber before returning to the auction room.

As the three men passed the open entrance door Jamouri poised for a second as he spotted an oncoming vehicle, denoted by a dust plume arising from the access road,

*"Look's like the first bidder is arriving."*

*"Excellent. Better break out the hubbles and whiskey for them"* ordered Gaber. Within a couple of minutes or so the black Hummer, a huge civilian jeep based on the American field jeep, took it's position alongside Jamouri's Merc and outstepped a dark skinned, bearded man in his late fifties dressed in a white djellaba escorted by a tall arab with a rifle slung over his shoulder.

Gaber recognised the man as Abdul-Jabbar, the war monger from the province of Batna in the north east of Algeria,

*"Salaam Abdul. Welcome you are the first to arrive so come on in"* Gaber beckoned.

*"Salaam Gaber. I hope you have better girls this time. The last one I bought had to be disposed of as she gave me so much trouble"* Abdul informed Gaber.

*"Oh yes, don't worry, there are some fabulous ones. Did you have any problem at the border post?"*asked Gaber.

*"No, sailed straight through."*

*"Good. I had arranged everything as usual"* responded Gaber.

It was then that a second and third dust plume appeared far down the road. The bastards for the auction were firmly on their way.

Within the hour no less than nine other Godfathers, of dubious reputations, had arrived including Tareek Amrouche from the Lllizi Province and Nabi Ulmalhansh from Mascara, two of the most feared bosses in Algeria. If the devil could, at this point, cast his net on the fortress of Tadla he would have quite a haul.

Then a noise of increasing amplitude, approached from the eastern sky. Instantly, Gaber knew who this was ...

Quasim Bin-Dahman, one of the richest and most ruthless men in Algeria. As the helicopter got closer the noise increased. Gaber ran out to the car park, where he expected the helicopter to land, in order to meet his special client. This was the man he hoped to negotiate a substantial sum from for supplying him with the white twins from England!

The dust flew everywhere as the Augusta AW119 aircraft touched down making it difficult for Gaber to keep his eyes open, even with his hands shielding his face. Eventually the blades ceased rotating and out stepped Bin-Dahman, dressed in a smart blue western suit and polished shoes together with the inevitable two heavily armed bodyguards but more importantly grasping a red leather briefcase.. This man had spent his life wheeling and dealing his way into a Government post within the Department of Imports which allowed him to 'financially benefit' from organising national contracts and had made a fortune with this long term association. For fear of their and their families lives few would dare to disagree or interfer  with his arrangement for business! Those that had were never seen again! His close connections with the Cosa Nostra in Sicily were well known. This was the Godfather of the Godfathers of the Algeria mafia.

*"Salaam Quasim. Welcome. Hope you had a good flight?"* Greeted Gaber with his outstretched hand.
*"Of course. "*
*"Would you take refresments first then meet the two special girls or sit in on the auction first?"* asked Gaber.
*"I will check out your specials  first, come to a deal, then enjoy your hospitality and will then sit in on the auction. You never know I might like one or two of them as well!"* Bin-Dahman informed Gaber.
*"No problem Quasim follow me."* Gaber ushered the balding and clean shaven Algerian through the main entrance and into a private room off to the right of the main hallway,
*"If you would care to just take a seat over there by the window whilst I will go and bring the girls up here for you to inspect"* Gaber

suggested.

*"Fine. My security can stand outside in the hall."*

Accompanied by Mohammed, Gaber opened the cell door allowing the light to once again cast it's rays upon the unfortunate girls held inside,

*"Mohammed fetch the two English girls and bring them with you to the main hall"* demanded Gaber. Immediately both Melika and Leyla felt this was the time that they may be parted so grasped hold of each other tightly in distress,

*"Come, you both come with me"* Mohammed instructed.

*"Fuck off you bastard. Go away and leave us alone!"* shouted Melika as she pulled her sister deeper into the wall recess.

Mohammed grabbed Melika's arm and pulled her towards the door.

*"Fuck off pig!"* she kept shouting as she hit Mohammed across the face. This act tighted Mohammed's grip and deepened his resolve to pull even harder. None of the other girls, all of whom were drugged to the limit, were in a position to help. All they could do was watch. Leyla then caught hold of the door frame which impeded their progress for an instant but Mohammed was a strong man and quickly overcame this punitive attempt to impede the progress towards the stairs. As they reached the hallway who should be there to greet them but Mido who leant across to Melika's ear and

whispered,

*"Remember what we agreed in the boat. Your buyer is one of the most important men in Algeria so will look after you. Consider yourself lucky as the other girls will be going through hell!"*

*"Is that supposed to make us feel good you fucking bastard"* Melika said as she spat in his face. Wiping the saliva away with his sleeve Mido again suggested they both behave for their own good.

Mohammed pushed the twins into the centre of the room, with Gaber and Mido gently following behind, then retiring outside to stand duty with Bin-Dahman's goons.

Immediately Gaber sauntered over to Bin-Dahman and suggested he have a closer inspection.

*"Bring them closer to me then!"* he demanded, to which Gaber  acknowledged and then went on to say,

*"They are English, around eighteen years old and best of all they are twins! What do you think Quasim?"*

Bin-Dahman bent forward and ran his large, hairy hands up Leyla's legs then underneath her djellaba before discovering she was not wearing any panties . At that point Leyla reacted by violently pulling her djellaba down almost forcing Bin-Dahman to the ground but remembering what Mido had said earlier she still could not hold back and just had to vent her anger,

*"Fuck off you perverted pig!"* she shouted .
*"Spirit! She has spirit Gaber."*

*"So what do you think then. Are they not the best I have ever offered you?"* Gaber asked nervously.

*"Ok Gaber you have done well, I cannot deny that. They are both the picture of beauty worthy to be the daughters of Allah himself. Bekam? (How much!)"* Bin-Dahman asked getting down to business with his usual direct approach. In order to justify his extortionate opening price Gaber continued with his complementary description and his explanation of the rarity value of the sisters,

*"Enough Gaber, you have sold me.. what's your price?"*

*" One million dollars Quasim."*

*"Mass zebbi maabol! (suck my dick crazy man!) one million! May Allah strike you dead Gaber. Half million?"*

*"You loose sight of the rarity of these two and the trouble I went too to acquire them for your pleasure........ seven hundred and fifty thousand?"* Gaber came back with.

*"I will make it six hundred and fifty thousand, my friend, final offer ..take it or leave it! Now bring me  some refreshments."*

*"Na'am mafi mushkila (yes ok no problem) I agree six hundred and fifty"* Gaber replied as his mouth widened with a satisfied grin of

contentment. His hand was then extended to commit to the deal. Bin-Dahman followed suit. Both men were happy. Gaber immediately requested that Mohammed take the girls back to their cell to await transfer to the Augusta helicopter when Bin-Dahman eventually left the auction.

---

All twenty five, fully armed, Surete personnel were stood to attention on the rear parade ground as Lieutenant Asan delivered his orders,

*"Men, we are going to attack the Fortress of Tadla to rescue several abducted girls that we believe are held there to be auctioned as sex slaves. This we cannot allow in Morocco! Be sure not to harm the women but the abductors I want dead or alive. We will attack from both front and rear entrances with three M151's at each entrance. I will indicate the start of our simultaneous attack with a green very pistol. Now to the jeeps and best of luck."*

The six jeeps, with Asan and Garcia in the lead, sped away in an acoustic cloud of dust from the station heading for the fortress. Despite the early evening hour the sun was beating down on the men in the open jeeps, each double checking their ammo magazines on the MAC 1950's and AK 47's were full and the safety catches set to OFF.

It took no more than twenty five minutes for the

group to halt at the junction where the road split for either the main or rear entrances,

*"Sergeant, you take your force up there to the rear and we will continue up here. Remember no shots to be fired till you see my green flare!"* Asan ordered.

Each group departed to take up their assault positions reducing their vehicle speed so as to reduce their dust signature cloud to a minimum. No point in telling the Algerians of their presence .. yet!

Some three hundred metres from the entrances all the M151's stopped, allowing the soldiers to dismount and disperse to take up various hidden vantage points for the assault. Within minutes all thirty one men were ready, poised with either their AK's or MAC's or pistols, for the attack ....... just waiting for Lieutenant Asan's green flare.

Chapter 11
_____**Let the selling begin**

As Gaber mounted the platform , a silence of anticipation befell the room and the assembled scurge of humanity gazed forewards to focus their attention on the imminent arrival of the girls and two boys for sale. Without any formal introduction to the gathering Gaber proceeded in Arabic,

*" Friends from Algeria welcome to the best auction yet. We have 9 girls and 2 boys for sale starting with this delightful young woman from Portugal."*

Mohammed assisted the semi-conscious girl up the four steps and paraded her back and forth across the stage so that all the assembled got a good look.

*"I will start the bidding at ten thousand dollars!"* Gaber continued.

*"Twelve"* came from the audience.

*"Fifteen."*

Then silence.

Gaber sensing a lull in the bidding then instructed Mohammed,

*"Mohammed, take of her cloak so they can see all that is for sale."*

Without the slightest objection from the girl Mohammed removed her djellaba leaving the wretched creature stark naked parading in front of the drouling assholes.

It did the trick and immediately the bidding continued,

*"Twenty thousand!" came from the back of the room.*

Eventually the bidding ceased at thirty five thousand dollars.

*"Sold for thirty five thousand dollars" Gaber announced as he brought down his ivory gabble.* It was Abdul-Jabbar who had bought the first offering. Mohammed escorted the sold girl

back down to the basement cell awaiting collection after she had being paid for.

*"Ok. Next we have a black haired Italian beauty. Come on gentlemen. For this one I will start you at twenty thousand. Do we have twenty?"* Gaber continued.

*"Twenty five!"*

Then from the middle of the room came another bid ,

*"Forty thousand dollars!"*

It was Nabi Ulmalhansh. Not wishing to loose out, Tareek Amrouche, the Godfather  from Lllizi, raised his voice,

*"Seventy thousand!"*

This bid confirmed his purchase. The third captive, another black haired beauty from Italy was brought up onto the stage by Mohammed and paraded around with his djellaba removed. With the precedent taken at seventy from the previous female and knowing the popularity for boys, Gaber opened the bidding,

*" Right, now we now have a beautiful boy, around fourteen years old from Italy and I will open at seventy five thousand."*

The hands raised and the shouting commenced.

*"Eighty thousand!"*
*"Eighty five!"*

The auctioning continued ................

Meanwhile, outside in the fortress courtyard Habib, one of the more vigilant bodyguard drivers, suddenly caught a glimpse of a flash of  a reflection of the descending sun glinting off the binoculars held up by Asan. With his attention now roused the driver  saw, for a brief second, the uniform of a Surete soldier dart from behind one of the orange trees. Then another. He immediately raised his walkie-talkie to contact his boss inside the auction room, Tareek Amrouche,

*"Boss, boss we have trouble. The Surete are closing in around the castle."*

*"Ebn El Sharmoota (son of a bitch)!"* Amrouche cried out for all to hear which disturbed the illicit gathering. It was at precisely this point that Lieutentant Asan sweezed the trigger of his very pistol releasing a bright green flare high into the sky. The signal had been given resulting in the immediate onslaught from the combined force of thirty or so soldiers from the Morroccan Surete and Spanish Guardia Civil.

*"Boss, boss, boss we are under attack from a large force get out now! We need to go now!"* shouted Habib into his radio. Amrouche took to his heels and rushed to the main entrance as fast as his feet would allow shouting,

*"we are under attack from the Surete get out everybody get out!"* as he did so. The unfolding drama soon led into a full scale panic as rifle shots ran out.

Bin-Dahman, who had the most too loose, ran like a demented dog on heat to find his bodyguards and ordered them to hastily collect his two girls, (Leyla and Melika) and bring them to the helicopter. Shots rang out from all quarters from both sides. The Surete as they edged their way toward to the fortress building and the bodyguards and drivers crouching behind the precious cars.

Zing, zing, zing as more and more Moroccan and Spanish bullets hit the brickwork and cars with glass crashing to the ground. Several men on both side took hits , some being fatal.

Bin-Dahman, having now safely manoeuvred his way to the helicopter amidst the hail of bullets and surrounded by his security guards, climbed aboard and ordered the pilot to quickly lit up the engine. Meanwhile  his two bodyguards had recovered the girls from the cell and were crossing the main hallway when Gaber ran across and demanded  payment in cash before their boss (Bin-Dahman) could leave with the girls.

*"Get out of my way"* shouted one of the guards as he pushed Gaber aside.

*"No no I want my money. Tell Bin-Dahman I want my money now!"* and tried to acost the guard.

Several bullets entered the pillars in the hallway ricocheting into the room. Gaber persisted with his assault on the guard who could delay no longer so reached into the inside of his cloak, withdrew his Smith and Wesson .40, aimed it at Gaber's temple and pressed the trigger. Gaber was dead before his bulky body hit the floor. Both Leyla and Melika, on seeing this as the best opportunity to escape, desparately fought and fought their hardest to break away from the guards whilst they were cowering down  in an attempt the lower their profile as a target for a Surete bullets, but to no avail, they were far too powerful and determined for the girls to overcome. By the time they reached the Augusta helicopter the blades were wizzing round creating another mini dust storm which in fact acted as a protective screen. With strict orders not to injure any of the girls none of the attacking soldiers was going to shoot blind into the cloud.

At the rear of the building the attacking force , having suffered only minor casualties, had breached the outer wall and were planting C4 explosive against the rear oak door ... bang! as the door disappeared in a smoke cloud. Several of the bodyguards and a couple of the bosses were waiting behind a stack of tables unleasing a hail of bullets into the oncoming Guardia and Surete soldiers as they poured through the now open doorway. Several hit the deck from their wounds.

At the main entrance some four of the Algerian buyers made it to their cars and attempted their escape at high speed only to be blown to bits in balls of fire by the Russian built RPG's launched by the waiting Surete.

Coronel Garcia just caught sight of the two girls as the cloud momentarily cleared being bundled into the helicopter,

*"The helicopter!"* he shouted in his loudest voice *"Get the helicopter. There are girls there so*

*shoot at the engine and fuel tank!"*
Melika had been tossed, by the guard, safely aboard in the rear of the plane, alongside Bin-Dahman and was at the point of throwing Leyla into the remaining spare seat when Garcia's revolver bullet entered the middle of the bodyguards back lodging in his spine with a result of instant unconsciousness. He reeled backwards to the ground leaving Leyla half in the plane grabbing the outer seatbelt as the pilot lifted off in the clouded confusion.

*"Help !! Help me Mel!"* Leyla screamed in total panic as the helicopter reached fifty feet above the ground with her hanging on for dear life to the seatbelt with her legs daggling outside the fuselage. Melika desparately grabbed her sisters hands in an attempt to pull her inside the cabin but Leyla was just too heavy.
*"Don't let me fall Mel. Please, please, please keep on holding me!"* Leyla cried as her grip on the seatbelt was loosening. Melika turned to Bin-Dahman,
*"Come on you bastard give me a hand. Help me save my sister!"*
*"No way. Just let her go. We have to get out of here"* he replied as he withdrew his .40 pistol from his shoulder holster.
*"No way you fucking pig!"* Melika screamed in pain as her hands began to loose strength. Three hundred feet and rising rapidly. Both girl's grips were loosening fast as the reality

of Leyla falling to her death was becoming inevitable.

*"Hold on, just hold on Leyla. For God's sake hold on!"* Melika cried out as she strained with all her might to hold her sister.

*"Let her go, damn it. We still have two hundred miles to go. Just let her go. Do a right hand bank pilot"* Bin-Dahman instructed. In a right bank Leyla hung out further from the fuselage of the Augusta.

*"You pissing bastard you're not even giving her a chance"* Mel shouted at the now panicing Algerian Politician.

*"Of course not she impeding our progress out of Moroccan airspace, now let her go, now!"* as he leant over to unlock Melika's handgrip.

*"Fuck off you bastard. I will do it now give me your gun. Give me your gun, now bastard! Damn you give me your gun, ....please! "* Melika pleaded with Dahman. Instantly he knew what action was about the follow and with a degree of self preservation foremost in his mind he reluctantly passed Melika his loaded revolver.
Looking her sister straight in the eye and with torrents of tears streaming down her cheeks Melika spoke to Leyla,

*"Forgive me my dear dear sister please forgive me for what I am about to do, as I cannot let you fall to an agonising death. I love you so much, forgive me"* and with her right hand, raised the pistol and aimed it at the centre

of Leyla's head.

*"No, no please no, Mel no I can hang on forever. I don't want to die. I love you Mel!!! I want to live!"*

Her hands began to loose grip and gently slide further down the seatbelt.

In a state of total torment and unbelievable emotional anguish Melika's right index finger gradually increased it's pressure on the trigger. The hammer released,

### "BANG"

Leyla's grip on the seatbelt released instantly, as the single bullet passed through her temple and exited from the back of the scull, allowing her body to tumble over and over in a sommersaulting pattern earthwards at an ever increasing rate until, after what seemed to be eternity, Melika saw her sister hit the sandy floor in a small cloud of sand and dust.

Melika, completely stunned with grief, took a few seconds to compose her emotions when Bin-Dahman made a grab to retrieve his revolver. With lighting reactions in her heightened state Melika swung round with the discerned intention of aiming the pistol at Bin-Dahman to kill him but by this time he had grabbed her arm which diverted the direction of the two bullets that left the pistol's short barrel. The first hit the pilot in his right shoulder, shattering his collar bone resulting in an excruciating pain and shock for him, and the second passed through the cabin headlining and severed the high pressure fuel feed line running from the injection pump to the combustion chamber of the one and only Pratt and Whitney turboshaft engine which immediately cut the flow of fuel to the engine whereby the windmilling effect of the descending rotors was all that was now keeping the Augusta in the air. As intended by design with all helicopters the Augusta descended rapidly in a spiral turn, normally with a certain amout of control from the pilot using his left hand for the cyclic lever and his right for the collective stick, however with his right arm and hand totally useless with the pain in his shoulder,

Bin-Dahman's pilot could not take control of the ensueing crash.

Coronel Garcia, still mixed up in the intense  fire fight several hundred feet below from his vantage point behind one of the jeeps, had previously glanced up and saw the body fall to its death and now the rapidly descending helicopter hurtling towards the ground.

*" Lieutenant bring two of your men and lets go over to the the helicopter in case there may be survivors."*

At that point a bullet from Ulmalhansh's bodyguard's rifle struck Garcia in the left leg, just above the knee, sending him to the ground.

*"Coronel you have been hit. Are you still alive?"* asked the concerned Lieutenant.

*"Yes i'm fine. It's just a flesh wound in the leg"* replied Garcia as he grasped the wound with both hands trying to hide the pain and gushing blood.

*"Can you walk? Hang on I will get one of the jeeps"* informed the rather excitable Asan and off he ran through a hail of bullets towards one of the Mi5i's.

Meanwhile in the Augusta all three occupants were becoming dizzy and disorientated in the spinning plane as the ground came hurtling towards them at an alarming rate.

*"Captain. Get control back now!!! before we crash!"* shouted Bin-Dahman.

*"I can't sir. I cannot move my right arm!"* cried out the pilot as he desparately fought the plane by only using his feet for yaw control and left hand for altering the prop pitch with the collective to control the rate of descent. He was doing his best and was exercising a certain amount of control, but not enough. The world screwed round and round for the three occupants as the 119 lost altitude in it's sprial descent. The engine had died completely through lack of fuel. The cabin went quiet except for the terrified screaming coming from Melika who by now was in a state of complete panic. Down and down went the Augusta, until "THUMP" as the slides (no wheels) suddenly dug into the sand bringing the helicopter to a sudden and dramatic halt throwing both it's unbelted passengers to

the floor.

Due to the inclined angle of touchdown, one after another the four rotating blades hit and dug into the soft sand becoming detatched from their shaft mountings as they did so.

There was silence, dead silence.

*"Come on Coronel get into the jeep. The helicopter has crash landed"* ordered the Moroccan Surete officer. With the help of the two soldiers, who had been seated in the rear, Garcia eventually manouvered his way into the front passenger seat and off sped the jeep in a cloud of dust with it's throttle held firmly to the floor by Asan's right foot.

Back in the Fortress the shooting was intense with bullets flying everywhere. Several bodies from both sides lay strewn on the floor. Some wounded and some, with their life extinguished resting in their own pools of blood. Mido had somehow made his way to the front entrance with the firm intention of making a dash for Jamouri's bulletproof Mercedes still parked in the courtyard on the other side of the oak walkway. Having seen his beautiful Range Rover receive a direct hit from an RPG ( Rocket propelled grenade) earlier, Jamouri's Merc had remained untouched so was the obvious car to make for. He saw Gaber's portly body lying on the floor and showed no sign of remorse or concern as he passed it by .. where was Jamouri?

Why should he care he thought to himself.

Not being a particularly fit or agile man, the run to the car was the longest and hardest exercise of Mido's sorry life, but he made it with several bullets spraying the sand around him as he approached the bridge and then splintering the wooden walkway as he crossed. Opening the drivers door he jumped into the seat and reached for the ignition key which fortunately was still in situ. Several more bullets hit the armoured windscreen but did no damage. Mido turned the key and instantly the reliable German 3.2 litre engine burst into life allowing Mido to move the drive selector to 'D' and hit the right pedal. The acceleration was profuse kicking up a cloud of dust and stones in it's wake as it headed down the twisty road back into Beni Mellal.

It took a bullet from one of the rear guard Guardia Civil soldiers, deployed to cut off those slavers that happen to break through the attack line, that entered the front right tyre of the Mercedes to render the steering unuseable and with Mido not being an accomplished driver fought hard to hold the car on the tarmac until it burst through the low stone wall and over the precipice. It took roughly six seconds of flight before coming to rest in scrub land bursting into a huge ball of flame. Mido was now history is his cremated German tomb.

Eventually , after having negotiated some rough ground and ascended a few mini sand dunes splattered with the ocassional ourcrops of rock,

Garcia's jeep arrived at the crash site to find the Augusta 119 sat upright, virtually intact, except for the four rotor blades stuck in the sand like the sentinel stones of stonehenge, but with no apparant movement from any of the occupants. Jumping from his seat Asan rushed to the rear cabin to find two bodies slumped on top of each other on the floor between the seat and forward bulkhead. With the help of his two soldiers Asan, realising that the male body on the top had to be one of the Algerian buyers, pulled it with no consideration of respect, out of the plane and dumped it on the sandy ground. However on finding the young female body underneath took a great deal of care and respect in retrieving her to a safe lying position on a soft sandy patch of ground. He felt for a pulse. There was one, but it was feint . She was alive. One of the soldiers then took the pulse of the male previously bundled in the sand.

*"This one is alive Lieutenant but only just"* the soldier advised.

*"Check the pilot"* ordered Asan.

The first view of the pilot with the cyclic stick firmly embedded into his face gave the soldier little hope of finding a pulse,

*"This one is dead sir."*

With the tiniest amount of body movement at first followed by the opening her her beautiful eyes Melika started to come round,

*"What happened. Who are you? Where am I?"* she asked to those assembled around her.

Garcia limped his way across to the female body,
*"Do you speak Arabic, French or English?"*
he asked.

*"English. I am English from London. Who are you?"* Melika requested.

*"I am Coronel Garcia from the Guardia Civil based at Marina Puerto Banus, Spain."*

*"Banus. Oh my God that is where we were a few days ago."*

*"Who's we?"* asked Garcia.

*"My sister Leyla and I."* Then the recollection of what had just happened started to hit her, Leyla, Leyla, the beautiful Leyla was lying out in the desert somewhere .

*"We must find Leyla. She eeeeeeerh fell out of the helicopter just before we crashed!"* Then, as the adrenaline kicked in and her eyes began to focus, Melika sat up and noticed something rather familiar edging it's way out of Garcia's right hand trouser pocket.

*"Is that what I am thinking it is in your pocket?"* she uttered.

*"What these?"* as Garcia pulled out a compact yellow bundle and handed it to Melika..

*"Oh God I was right they are Leyla's panties with our message in lipstick still written on them. You found them? It worked!"* bursting into tears.

*"Some fishermen found them floating in the sea off Gibraltar"* Garcia informed her.

163

*"We must find her. She must come home with me"* Melika pleaded.

Meanwhile, the other soldier was checking through the pockets of the breathing male body for identification. Withdrawing the ID card from his upper inside pocket and opening it brought an expression of surprise to the soldiers face,

*"I now know this man Sir, he is Quasim Bin-Dahman, a leading politician in the Algerian Government. He was on TV the other night supporting a trade deal between us and Algeria."*

*"What! What the hell is he doing here?"* asked Lieutenant Asan in complete surprise.

*"He's the bastard who bought me and Leyla!"* Melika informed Asan.

*"What him! Dahman buying slaves and on Moroccan soil. Allah! This will be very embarrassing for both our Governments! What are we going to do with him?"*

*"We must go and find the other girl before the desert foxes find her!" Garcia* shouted out loud so all the assembled could hear.

Realizing that an ugly and embarrassing diplomatic situation would most certainly occur if Bin-Dahman was to be put on trial in Rabat, for buying slaves, Lieutenant Asan felt he had to make one of the most difficult decisions of his military career .. Once he had overseen Coronel Garcia, Melika and the two soldiers sat in the jeeps ready for the off to find Leyla's body he

(Asan) walked over to the still unconscious Bin-Dahman and with his back shielding his actions from the occupants of the jeep, bent down, lifted Bin-Dahman's head clear from the ground before slamming it back down with all the strength he could muster resulting in a dull cracking sound followed by a large flowing of cranial blood. Asan felt confident that Mr Bin-Dahman was now dead and that it would look like he had received his fatal injuries from the helicopter crash. Eventually the body could be returned to Algeria with no need for a humiliating public trial.

Having taken up the front passenger seat of the lead jeep Asan then ordered the convoy north to where it was assumed Leyla's body might still be lying.

Back at the fortress an end to the shooting seemed in sight as one after the other  the remaining buyers, their drivers and bodyguards threw down their weapons, raised their hands into the air and walked out of the smoking building. The combination of Surete and Guardia Civil had proved too dominant for the not too well prepared Bosses from Algeria.

With Lieutenant Asan away at the crash site, Sergeant Hussein, now being the senior Surete soldier at the fortress, assumed command and ordered the captives to be lined up against the outer wall in preparation for a firing squad. Of course the final order for the executions would have to come from Lieutenant Asan upon his return so until then Hussein had ten of his men facing the prisoners with their rifles poised at the ready.

It did not take long driving across the rugged terrain of eastern Morocco for Asan to spot the inevitable flock of bald-headed vultures cruising high in a circle above what they took to be their next meal.

*"Over there, there's something over there at the bottom of that wadi. Can you see it Coronel?"* Asan asked.

*"You mean that bundle that looks like a rock?"*

*"Yes, let's go."*

Gingerly edging it's way down the gentle but rocky slope to the wadi floor the two jeep convoy eventually drew up beside the broken and half buried body of a white female. Immediately Melika recognised the djellaba her sister had been wearing but it was not until she saw the disjointed, crumpled and bloody corpse that had been ripped apart by the ravinous foxes, but more profoundly the look of horror cemented on the face, that Melika felt a spear pierce her heart in sorrow, sadness and finally guilt as it was her persuation that encouraged them both to holiday together in Marbella in the first place. .

Dropping to her knees to cuddle what was left of her sister for one last time Melika could not hold back the torrents of tears now flooding from her eyes. Melika's head fully dropped to her chest in utter remorse.

Asan, full of sympathy and remorse himself for the demise of the poor girl, bent over to comfort the grieving English girl when he noticed the neat round entry hole in the centre of the dead girl's head. Immediately suspecting foul play he carefully and respectfully rotated the head to discover the ragged exit wound at the rear with much of the brain tissue still gently ouzing out. It took a few moments of deep thought for him to interpret the situation .. the girl must surely have been alive when she got into the helicopter so it could only have been one of the other occupants on board that could have committed this atrocity .....either the pilot, Bin-Dahman or the sister .. *"but why?? or maybe a stray bullet from one of the soldiers? "* he thought to himself.

Standing up to his full height he thought more .. *"the pilot had to be ruled out as he would have been far too busy flying the plane and a stray soldiers bullet .. well it would have to have been a rifle shot but the small size of the entry hole was that of a pistol!. Bin-Dahman was the obvious suspect, but why, why when he had just bought her?"* kept running through Lieutenant Asan's mind. Reluctantly he requested that Melika stand up and face him,

*"I'm sorry to intrude on your period of sorrow but can you tell me precisely what happened in the helicopter after take-off?"*

*"Of course"* Melika continued whilst trying to wipe away the tears.

*"We were both bundled into the plane ............................................................................................... I could not let Leyla fall, alive, and see the ground coming up towards her so I shot her, as you would shoot a lame horse. After that ..............we crashed into the desert"* Melika recounted in a slow and deliberate way.

*"Oh no, oh no. So you shot her in cold blood?"* Asan asked Melika to confirm.

*"Well I suppose so, but what other choice did I have?"* she replied.

Reaching behind his back for the pair of stainless steel handcuffs, which dandled from his belt, the Surete Lieutenant gently placed Melika's hands within the cuffs before clasping them shut,

*" I have to place you under arrest for the murder of your sister who now lies before you. I have to advise you that if you go to trial in Casablanca and are found guilty you will be taken to a public place and either shot by a firing squad or beheaded. Now you will come with me to the station in Beni Mellal"* Lieutenant Asan continued in his capacity of the law representative

The instantaneous reaction from Melika was predictable,

*"You must be joking!! I loved my sister that's why I sent her to sleep. Don't you understand!!"* Melika pleaded in a voice of disbelief.

*"Yes I do, but it will be up to the jury to understand, not me"* Asan replied. It was then that the Spanish Coronel, who having stood next to Asan during the arrest, intervened,

*"Lieutenant. Whilst we all agree that the law must be upheld this cannot be sane justice. There has to be another way"* he suggested.

*"I agree with your sentiments Coronel but we have our law to observe, however, give me a few minutes to think this situation through"* Asan stated as he paced backwards and forwards, backwards and forwards     several times in deep thought. Meanwhile Melika, once again, sank to her knees in prayer for her dear departed sister.

*"I have it! There is a way!"* shouted Asan as he started to gather together the grieving Melika and Coronel Garcia  for a confidential and 'illegal' chat whilst ordering  the two escorting soldiers to return and have a search of the wreckage for any guns, money or valubles.

*"There is a way out of this if the three of us agree to it. It's not pleasant, it will not be easy but it will work"* continued Asan.

"What is it? Please tell me" *asked Melika.*

*" Ok, are you ready for this? We bury your sister's body, very, very deep right over there by that rock so that she will never, ever be found and leave a fragment of her djellaba, way over there in the opposite direction, which will eventually be found by those coming to search*

*for evidence, later on, to confirm that your sister was taken and consumed by desert foxes."*

Then turning to Melika said,

*" It will mean that you will not have a body to escort home to England."*

*" But I have to take her home. Mum will want to bury her."* Melika insisted.

*"I understand but if you want to be free that cannot happen. The choice is yours. I can give you ten minutes to think about it"* Asan advised her and walked away to sort out about getting the two male corpses, still at the wreckage site, into the jeeps.

Pacing round and round in a tight but controlled circle with her hands still  in cuffs, with anguish thoughts about which of the two evils she should agree too, pulsated through her head before Melika finally came to a decision. The thought of languishing in a Moroccan jail for maybe months before possibly being executed in public only just outweighed the fact that Leyla would have to rest hidden in the Moroccan desert without any funeral.

*"Well what have you decided?"* Asan asked having decided to  stack the bodies at the wreckage into one of the  jeeps and return them to the fort for disposal.

With tears again pouring down her cheeks Melika raised her head,

*"We bury my dear sister here."*

*"Best decision all round I think"* commented Garcia,

*"At least your freedom to go home and comfort your mother will then be guaranteed."*

*"Ok . Let's get on with it as time is running out"* spoke Asan in a demure tone before removing  the spades from the jeep for them to dig a hole at least three metres deep over by the assigned rock.

It took the best part of an hour for the two men to excavate a large enough grave in the free running sand. Then afterwards Coronel Garcia and Melika, with the cuffs now removed, tried their best to tidy up  Leyla's corpse, having torn off a section of the djellaba and then wrapped the remains of the body up in a Moroccan flag that happened to be stowed in the lead jeep.

With either end tightly held by one of the soldiers whilst being watched by the Melika, the corpse was carefully and respectfully lowered into the deep grave. Filling it in was considerably easier and quicker than digging it out which was followed with the final placing of several stones over the site to camouflage the grave's location diligently carried out by Asan and Melika. All the assembled then stood to attention around the site before bowing their heads in a moments silent prayer.

*"Goodbye dear Leyla, please forgive me. I will tell mum the truth and one day bring her to see you, I promise. Forgive me. Bye, bye darling"* Melika whispered and burst into an

uncontrollable fit of crying.

Garcia wrapped his arms around her shoulders and escorted Melika back to the lead jeep which was then carefully driven back to the fortress by Asan having first met up with the other jeep carrying the bodies from the helicopter wreckage.

Pulling up to the fortress footbridge it was immediately obvious to the two officers, through the absence of any gunfire, that the battle was over and  the sight of one of the Surete soldiers running across the bridge to greet his returning commander confirmed that the Algerian buyers had been beaten. Having just left a scene of severe depression this news of victory brought a rye smile to Asan's face.

*"Are there any prisoners?"* Asan asked of his now 'out of breath' soldier and *"What of the abducted girls, are they safe and sound?*

*"Yes sir, there are no casualties with the women and two boys. They are in shock and all need immediate hospital treatment for drug abuse. We have  twelve  prisoners lined up against the wall over there awaiting your orders, Sir"* the soldier reported.

*"Very well get onto the hospital and get all their vehicals and spare staff up here now and get some men to help you carry these two bodies to the entrance . Now where are the prisoners did you say?"* Asan ordered.

Having arranged for the two soldiers that were in the jeeps to stay with Melika, Asan and Garcia made their way to the  scene of carnage in front of the fortress. It was not a pretty sight that befell them with burnt out cars, some still on fire, broken glass and bullet shells strew over the ground but worse of all several bodies lying in their own pools of blood.

*"Did we suffer any casualities"* Asan asked one of his men.

*"One dead and two injured. No Guardia casualties at all Sir."*

*"Could have been worse. Well done."*

Now it was time for Asan to make a decision about the prisoners which prompted him to take a preview and a stocktake of those still being held against the wall . Whilst pacing up and down in front of the Algerian and ocassional Moroccan thugs Asan asked each in turn what part they played in the auction and abductions allowing them an opportunity to confess and implicate those who were in control. For fear of loosing face or of retribution to either themselves or their families no-one ventured any information, however, when questioning the well dressed prisoner standing at the far end of the line-up, a response whispered into Asan's ear, was forthcoming,

*"Lieutenant. I know you have a job to do and it appears that you have done it well,*

*however, I am sure that your family would be grateful for a better standard of living. I am Youssef Jamouri and have a million dollars available for you if my freedom can be guaranteed?"*

Jamouri was sure that Lieutenant Asan could be bought, afterall all the other officials that had presented any form of problem in the past had been ameanable to a few American greenbacks.

After a moments thought Asan then remarked,

*"Interesting. Ah! Your the man from the nice house in Casablanca and the owner of the boat "Ria Jacoba"? Where is this million dollars then and how could I be sure that I get it all"* he asked Jamouri, as if he was interested.

*"Get me away from this scum and I will tell you."*

*"Ok, move over there by that black BMW and we will talk in a minute"* Asan advised Jamouri. Once Jamouri was safe out of the way and reassurringly resting on the bonnet of the black 735, Asan had summed up his options over the fate he had in mind for the rest of the prisoners. To arrest them all and have a public trial would take quite a long time and without doubt, due to the standing in Algerian society of some of the bosses, it could easily create an international scene and even the possiblility of acquittal could be arrived at to soften the already delicate relations with Algeria. For the disgusting crimes they had committed Asan was not going to allow this possibility to be presented. As the

senior Surete officer in this part of Eastern Morocco he was happy to be accountable to Rabat HQ for what he was about to do.

Standing to the side of the line up of his soldiers, still wielding their rifles at the prisoners standing patiently against the wall, the Lieutentant shouted out his order,

*"Present your weapons, **Fire**!"*

The echoing of twelve rifle shots rang round the courtyard as the eleven bodies dropped to the floor, then in true military style Asan withdrew his pistol from it's holster, walked over to the bodies and put a single bullet into each of their heads to ensure death was certain. The sudden crescendo of gunfire rippled through Melika's body with a tinge of delight creeping into her facial expression. The bastards that were respsonsible for Leyla's death were now themselves dead.

Before attending to the needs of Jamouri, Asan ordered that all the bodies of those involved in the abduction and auctioning of the captives, including those from the wrecked helicopter, be piled up in a heap in the centre of the courtyard and for a couple of jerry cans of petrol to be brought over from some of the jeeps.

This done he further ordered that all the petrol be poured over the bodies.

Then walking over to and standing beside the smerking Jamouri, Asan said to him,

*"You can see what is about to happen. So*

*tell me where abouts is this money for me?"*
  *"In my house of course ."*
  *"Where in your house?"*
Before he realised what he was saying Jamouri
answered,
  *" In the floor safe in the conservatory."*
Then without any due thought or compulsion
Asan lifted his revolver to Jamouri's head and
thanked him.......... before pulling the trigger.
  *"Take this disgusting body and put it on
top of the heap"* he then ordered of two of his
soldiers.
This done Asan then suggested that all the
Surete and Guardia soldiers together with
Coronel Garcia and all the now freed abductees
gather around the heaped bodies at a safe
distance,
  *"Let this be a lesson to any who would
consider getting involved in this illegal and
unacceptable  crime,"* then turning to the soldier
to his right said,
  *" Throw a match and put an end to this
obsenity."*
**Whooosh** as the fuel immediately ignited
sending a putrid, burning smell of human flesh
high into the atmosphere for all of Beni Mellal to
observe. It was not until the pyre was in full
flame that Asan suddenly realised that several of
the bodies would have had copious amounts of
cash about them. Too late, for it was now gone,
however he ordered a full search of all the cars
and the fortress in the unlikely event some my
still be found. His luck was in as hidden in the

glove compartment of the white Lexus was a leather wallet containing some one hundred thousand very tatty, American dollars and stowed in the spare wheel section of the  black S class Mercedes boot was a further two hundred thousand or so American dollars. It would seem that the international currency in the slavery trade was the good all-American greenback. Once it was all safely in his possession Asan called all the men, both Moroccan and Spanish, together for a final briefing.

 Standing on the rear seat of one of the jeeps he commenced his delivery,

*"Men. The details of this tragic and disgusting day are to be forgotten but the penalty for trafficking must NOT!. I have here the remains of the cash from the traders and I hereby pledge half of it to go to the family of our fallen comrade, Private Hassan, who will be buried with full honours in due course and the other half to go towards rehabilitating the unfortunate women and boys who were abused. Now I  have arranged for them to be transported to the hospital where they will be looked after, in fact I can hear the ambulances arriving , so all of you return to you duties or families and on behalf of the abused who you all saved .. a big, big thankyou."*

Asan then jumped from the jeep and headed for Coronel Garcia and Melika who were standing together.

*"Coronel, Sir, this disgusting business is now concluded. I assume you will be escorting the English girl back to Spain, but I want you to call in at Jamouri's house en-route and in the conservatory floor safe you will find one million dollars. Get it and give it to the English girl for her and her family. It might help!"*
Then turning to Melika said,
*"Dear young lady, on behalf of my Government I apologise to you for the loss of your sister and the disgusting behaviour shown to you by several of my fellow countrymen. From my actions of today you can see that this behaviour is not acceptable. I hope you understand."*
Gathering his men together, having concluded his appreciation of Lieutenant Asan's help and assistance, Coronel Garcia ushered them back to his two jeeps in readiness to return to Casablanca and the awaiting Rodman in the port which will carry them back to Puerto Banus in Spain.
The abduction scenario was now concluded.


The complimentary flight back to London from Malaga, into the waiting arms of her mother and father, would be the longest, loneliest and saddest of Melika's entire life.

**The Fortress of Tadla**

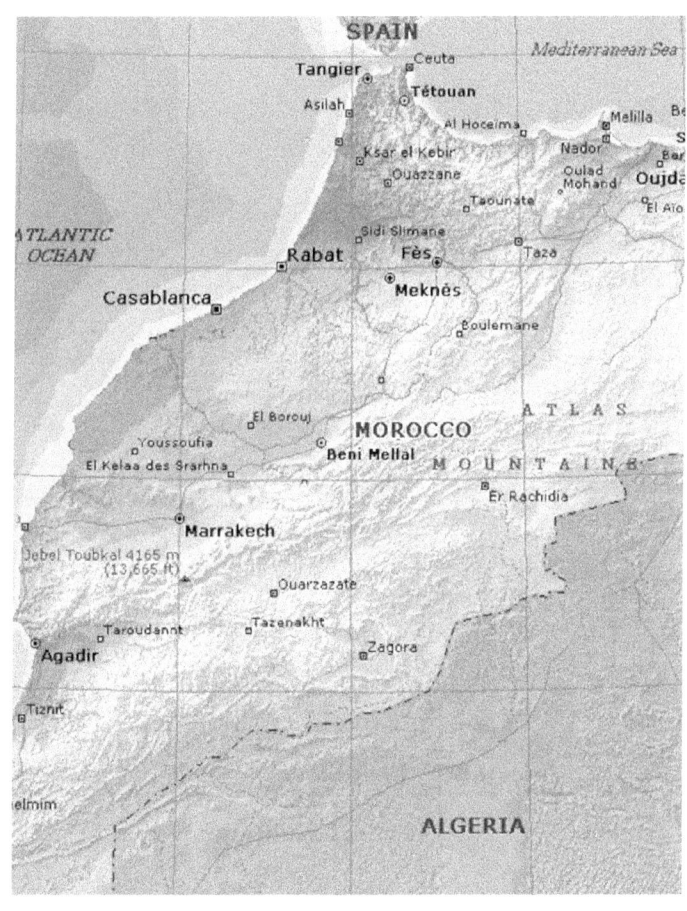

**Port of Casablanca**

**Augusta AW119 helicopter**

The **"An Appointment"**
series of paperbacks
by Jon Grainge
all available as **e-books** on either

**www.blurb.com/user/store/hightrainman**
(for Apple ipad and ipod)

New books:
**C ounter-Strike**
**A Voice from Heaven**
**Echoes from a Silent Enemy**
**Fateful Decision**

Appointment in **DOUZ**

Appointment with a
**FAITH**

Appointment in **CAIRO**

Appointment in
**Puerto Banus**

The
# "EUROPEAN PHOTO-BOOK"
collection
by Jon Grainge

A unique library of specialist titles of on-line
Photo-Books for the connoisseur

Available on:
www.blurb.com/user/store/hightrainman
as **e-books**
for Apple Ipad or Iphone

## Appointment in **Puerto Banus**      "Double Abduction"

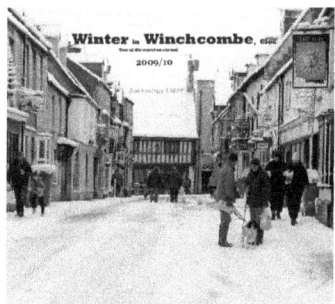

**"Winter in Winchcombe"**

**"574.8 Kilometers per Hour"**

**"Air Tattoo 2009-2012"**

**"2013/14 The Future Begins"**

**"Cocktails and Shots"**

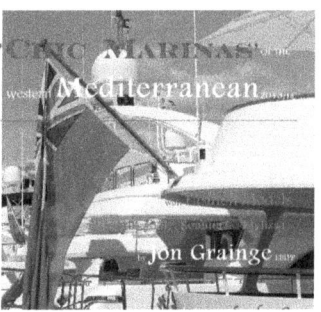

**"CHIC MARINAS"**
of the western Mediterranean

189

Lightning Source UK Ltd.
Milton Keynes UK
UKHW022207101221
395468UK00009B/512/J